York doesn't know what he's doing with the clan. He kidnapped a clan member, kept him under a spell, and almost killed him. Why did the clan welcome him with open arms and forgive him when he can't forgive himself? How can they stand to look at him when he's useless?

But maybe he doesn't have to be.

Leo has kept an eye on York since he moved in with the clan. York had kidnapped Leo's best friend, but if Marcel can forgive him, so can Leo. The fact that York is adorably cute and vulnerable helps, and when Leo allows him in, it doesn't take him long to start falling for him.

York wants everything the clan and Leo are offering, but he needs to give them more in return. The only thing he can think of is to go to Curt, the clan's enemy, and attempt to fool him into giving him information.

When Curt sees right through York and locks him up, York realizes how stupid his plan is. He's away from the clan, unable to free himself and completely alone.

Or is he?

A Psychic in Need
Copyright © 2023 Catherine Lievens
ISBN: 978-1-4874-3776-3
Cover art by Angela Waters

Published by eXtasy Books Inc

Look for us online at:
www.eXtasybooks.com

A Psychic in Need
It's a Psychic World 4

By

Catherine Lievens

CHAPTER ONE

York could hear people walk past his bedroom door. It was almost dinner time, and he held his breath, wondering if someone would knock.

He wouldn't be surprised if they did. Most of the clan hadn't tried talking to him and usually stared at him from afar, but a few clan members had made a point of trying to befriend him. He wasn't sure why, but he knew it was better if he stayed away from them.

He didn't deserve their friendship. Hell, he didn't deserve to be here, safe and with a roof over his head, after what he'd done. He didn't understand why Tim and Marcel, along with Marcel's parents, seemed to want him to truly become part of the clan. It didn't make sense, but he was too afraid to ask.

It was much easier to hide in his bedroom.

He looked around the room from where he was curled on the window seat. He hadn't understood what was happening when he'd been brought here. It didn't make sense to him that the clan was offering him a place to live after what he'd done. He doubted anyone else would have been welcomed into the clan after kidnapping one of their members and almost killing him, yet here he was.

But he was terrified.

The clan hadn't done anything to hurt him, and he didn't think they would. He might not understand them, but they seemed like good people. Maybe that was why they were so ready to give him a second chance. *He* wasn't giving himself a second chance, so it was odd. He hoped to make it easier for everyone by staying in his bedroom, but he also felt guilty. They were giving him so much, and he wasn't giving them anything in return. The very least he could do was make himself useful, but how?

He sighed and turned back to look out the window, where he could see Leo finishing up his work in the yard.

What could York do? He'd told the clan everything he knew about Curt, but as far as he was aware, they still didn't know where he was hiding. There was nothing else York could do, so maybe he should leave.

It would make life easier for everyone but himself, but he deserved not to have a home and a family. The only family he'd ever had was his brother, and Cooper was gone. He was the reason York had done what he'd done, and even though York regretted hurting Marcel, if it meant he'd eventually get Cooper back, he'd do it again. His brother would hate him if he found out, but York was starting to wonder if he ever would.

He pushed that thought away. He never allowed himself to dwell on it, not even when he was all alone in the darkness of the night. He *would* find Cooper. He had to convince himself of that because if he couldn't, all of this would have been pointless. He'd have hurt Marcel for nothing, and he didn't think he could live with that.

He sucked in a breath and closed his eyes. He had no idea what he was doing, but he knew it was possible for a psychic to pull a ghost toward them. He'd seen other psychics do it, and he'd been convinced Curt would teach him how to do the same. He should have known better, but he'd been desperate.

And he still was.

He thought of Cooper and how his brother had protected him after their parents passed. He thought of how warm his brother had been, how loving, of how Cooper had made sure York had everything he needed, even if it meant not having it himself. It had taken York some time to see it, but now, he knew that sometimes, Cooper had gone without food so that he could have it. Cooper had kept York safe, and then, he'd died.

York ignored that thought, too, and focused on his brother again. He tried to make the image in his mind as realistic as he could, even thinking of the way Cooper used to tuck his hair behind his ear and smile. Then he imagined having Cooper in front of him, pulling him into his arms and hugging him for the first time in years. He held his breath as he opened his eyes, but the room was empty except for him.

York stopped smiling.

He thumped his forehead against the cold window. He should have known it wouldn't work. He wasn't a great psychic, and he didn't have any training. Victor, an experienced psychic who worked with the clan, had offered to teach him, but York didn't want to take advantage of him. He was tempted, though. It might be the only way for him to get Cooper back, and he'd do anything to make that happen.

A knock on his door startled him. He stared at it as if it might burst, but that wasn't what happened. Instead, the person on the other side knocked again, and York knew that whoever it was wouldn't leave until he talked to him.

He licked his lips and got up from the window seat. He'd been in that position for so long that his legs felt wobbly, but he ignored it as he went to the door and put his hand on the handle. He sucked in a breath and slowly opened it, wondering what was about to happen.

No one in the clan had mistreated him, but he wouldn't be surprised if they eventually had enough of him and decided to kick him out. After all, he'd kick himself out if he were in their position. Cooper had been the nice one between them. York was uncomfortable with most people and had done something he could never atone for.

Opening the door revealed Tim standing on the other side. He'd raised his hand to knock again, but he quickly lowered it when he saw York and grinned at him.

"Victor and I are going to dinner. Are you coming with us?"

York wasn't hungry, but he needed to eat. Still, he could think of nothing worse than having to eat dinner with the clan. What if everyone stared at him? Or maybe tried to kick him out?

He wasn't even sure why he wondered about, that because no one had done anything like that since he'd arrived. Several people had stared as if they expected him to do something, but he didn't blame them for that, considering what he had done.

"It's probably better if I stay here," he murmured.

"I'll bring you food if you'd rather stay, but I think it would be good for you and the clan if you came downstairs."

"Why would it be good for the clan?" York understood why it would be good for him, at least from Tim's point of view.

It was kind of terrifying to be surrounded by dragons who could eat him with one bite, though. He hoped humans didn't taste that good and that no one would be tempted to do exactly that.

"Because you're a clan member. That means you're one of us, but it's hard to wrap our mind around that when you're never around."

York swallowed, trying to find something to say. "I don't think I'm really a clan member," he eventually settled on. "I'm not going to stay here forever." If he could, he'd leave now, but he didn't think the dragons would allow him to do that. He might still know something about Curt that he hadn't told them, so he understood and wasn't offended. He had no more information, but it made sense they didn't believe him.

4

Tim frowned. "You are. There's no ceremony or anything like that, but we all consider you a clan member. Besides, you live with us now."

"What about everyone else? Victor and his brothers, Jerome, Lindsey, and Will? As far as I know, they never belonged to the clan. They're here because it's too dangerous for them to live away from the clan, and there's safety in numbers, but I'm sure that once this is over, they'll go home."

"Maybe, maybe not. Even if they do leave, it doesn't mean they won't be clan members anymore. You don't have to live with the clan to belong." Tim hesitated. "And I'd understand if you decided to leave. We're nothing to you, even though I consider you a friend. I believe you should give the clan a chance, though. If you did, you'd be able to see we're not horrible people."

"I never thought you were. You gave me a chance when no one else would have."

"We gave you a chance because you deserve one. I know you don't have anyone else. You could give us a chance and see what happens."

How could York say no to that? Tim sounded convinced of what he was saying, and York felt he should give him and the rest of the clan everything they wanted. After everything they'd done for him, it was the least he could do, wasn't it? He didn't know how this evening would end, if maybe someone would tell him to leave and that he didn't belong, but he supposed he was about to find out. Tim was too sweet, and York couldn't keep saying no to him.

He sighed and looked back at his bedroom. "I'll come."

The way Tim's eyes lit up almost made York smile back. Almost.

Leo quickly made his way inside the house. He needed to

clean up before going to dinner, but he was starving, and he hoped the rest of the clan would leave him something to eat.

He went upstairs to his bedroom, nodding at several people he crossed paths with as he did so. A few tried talking to him, but he gestured at his dirty clothes, and they understood. He worked outside, keeping the yard clean and healthy, and the clan benefited from that. Leo was proud of the work he did, even though sometimes, he didn't feel as useful as some of the other dragons in the clan. He didn't *need* to be useful in other ways, though. If he wasn't working on the yard, it would be a mess. What he did suited him, so he was more than happy to continue.

He rushed through his shower, then quickly threw on a clean pair of jeans, a sweater, socks, and shoes. He grabbed his phone, then made his way downstairs.

He could hear the noises of many people in the dining hall, talking and laughing, the ding of their silverware hitting their plates, adding a slight music. He looked around when he walked in, hoping someone had saved him a chair, not one bit surprised when Marcel waved at him. He waved back, and Marcel pointed at the chair next to him. It was empty, while the one on his other side had his boyfriend.

Leo gave his friend a thumbs up, then headed toward the long tables that held the food. They were full of half-empty metal pans, and he quickly filled his plate with everything he craved, including macaroni and cheese, broccoli, and steak. He could see the kitchen behind the tables, and he winked at Palmer, one of the cooks. Palmer's cheeks flushed, but he grinned back before turning to the food he was preparing, and Leo made his way toward the table where Marcel was sitting.

By the time he reached it, it was to find that most of the table was full. Tim and Victor were there, but they weren't who caught Leo's attention.

That was all York.

Leo narrowed his eyes at the psychic, briefly wondering what he was doing here before shaking himself. York was here because he was a clan member, and it was his right to have dinner with the rest of the clan. Whatever he'd done in the past, Elijah had seen something in him that had pushed him to welcome him into the clan, and even after what York had done to Marcel, Leo found that he agreed with Elijah.

Something about the psychic made him want to reach for him. Maybe it was because York appeared fragile or because Leo was sure that Curt had taken advantage of how vulnerable York had been when his brother died. Leo didn't have siblings, but he'd almost lost Marcel, and they'd been friends for so long that it would have been like losing a brother. He could understand how York felt and why he'd done what he'd done.

That didn't mean he wouldn't keep an eye on him.

"I wasn't sure you'd be in time for dinner," Marcel said as he smiled at Leo.

Leo sat next to him and bumped their shoulders together. "Are you kidding? I'm starving. I wouldn't miss dinner even if you paid me."

Marcel laughed. Leo didn't miss the way York peeked at him, but York noticed him looking and quickly looked back down at his plate.

He was sitting next to Tim, and Tim leaned closer to whisper something to him. It made York smile slightly, and Leo found himself wondering what Tim had said. It was none of his business, but he wanted to find out anyway.

York was none of his business. Now that Marcel was back, Leo could stay away from the psychic, and it would probably be better if he did just that. But Leo knew himself, and for some reason, he was fascinated by York. He understood York's pain, albeit not entirely. He wanted to soothe it and show him that he wasn't alone in the world, but he'd kept his distance. It was clear that York felt uncomfortable in the middle of so many dragons, and he probably expected the other shoe to drop. Leo knew he would be in his place.

"Leo?" Marcel asked, poking between Leo's ribs with a finger.

Leo leaned away and glared at his friend. "What?"

"You weren't listening to me."

"Sorry. I was distracted."

Marcel's gaze flickered to York, who was still staring at his plate as if it was the most interesting thing in the world. "By York?" Marcel asked in a whisper.

Leo considered lying to his best friend, but Marcel knew him too well, and besides, why should he lie? Marcel wouldn't care that Leo found York interesting. "Yeah."

Just like Leo had expected, Marcel smiled. "He's an interesting person. Have you tried talking to him?"

"When would I have? I've been busy, and as far as I can tell, he stays in his bedroom."

"I can't say I blame him. It has to be terrifying to be in the middle of a dragon clan, especially after everything that already happened to him." Marcel leaned even closer. "Are you interested in him?"

"Of course not," Leo said before he could think better of it.

He wasn't ashamed of the fact that he found York interesting and cute, but Leo didn't know if he could forgive him for what he'd done to Marcel. No doubt that made him an asshole, since Marcel himself had forgiven York, but he couldn't help how he felt.

"You know it wouldn't be a problem if you liked him, right?" Marcel asked. His tone was gentle, as if he feared Leo wouldn't take it well.

"How did you forgive him?" Leo asked instead of answering.

"How could I not? He was trying to save his brother, and I'd do pretty much anything to save you and Jerome."

"Your brother isn't dead."

"So? York is a psychic. I can only imagine how hard it is for him not to be able to see his brother when he can see other dead people. Besides, he didn't want to hurt me. That was all Curt, and he's the only one I hold responsible for what happened to me. That's why I wouldn't have a problem if you like York. I want him to feel at home here, and maybe you could help with that."

"Are you throwing me at him so he'll stay?" Leo was teasing, but Marcel's expression was solemn as he nodded.

"Maybe it's what he needs. He's been lonely, even though I don't think he'd admit that to anyone, least of all me. He deserves a lot more than he has, and if I could give him back his brother, I would. Unfortunately, Cooper is dead, but that doesn't mean York can't find someone else to love and to be his family. Maybe if he finally realizes no one here blames him for what happened, he'll be able to relax."

Leo looked at York again. He was on the other side of the table, focused on his plate, even though he was surrounded by people who could be his friends. It hurt Leo to see him like that, but could he really change things?

Marcel sighed. "I can see you're thinking, and that's always dangerous."

Leo glared at him. "Are you saying I have stupid ideas?"

"A lot of the time, but you also have good ideas, and maybe this is one of those. Just take it slow, all right? He's incredibly fragile, and I'm pretty sure he's ready to bolt if you spook him."

"Maybe he *should* go. It's clear he's not comfortable with us."

"But that doesn't mean we have to give up on him. Besides, it's not safe for him to be out there on his own right now. He'll have to stay with the clan until this Curt thing is over, and I hope that by the time it is, York will realize that he's already home and that he doesn't need to leave."

Leo didn't understand why, but he agreed with Marcel. York was home as much as he was, and maybe, it was time to show York that. Leo had no idea how he'd do it, but he'd find a way.

He always did.

The food had been great, but York was relieved dinner was over. Tim was busy with Victor, so York quickly got to his feet, grabbed his plate, and snuck away. He left his plate with the others on the tables by the kitchen, then walked toward the exit as quickly as he could. If he was lucky, he'd be back in his bedroom by the time anyone realized he was gone.

He wasn't lucky.

A woman stepped in front of him, and he had to stop. He couldn't ignore Marcel's mother, even though the thought of talking to her made him panic. What did she want? It would be her right to be angry at York and tell him she never wanted to see him again and that he didn't deserve anything the clan was giving him, but York had already met her. He knew that wasn't how she felt and what she'd say, even though he didn't understand why she seemed so happy to see him.

She beamed at him and grabbed his wrist. "It was so good to see you at dinner," she said. "I didn't think it was you in the beginning, but that's because you've been spending a lot of time in your room. Are you done with that?"

York had no idea how to answer that question. He couldn't say no because she'd get worried and want to help, but if he said yes, it would be a lie.

"Leave the poor man alone," her husband said as he wrapped an arm around her shoulders.

She dropped York's wrist, but she didn't leave. "I'd leave him alone if he spent more time out of his bedroom. I just don't want him to be afraid of dragons." She looked at York. "You know we won't hurt you, right? And we don't eat humans." She wrinkled her nose. "Usually. They're hard to digest."

A few months ago, York would have been terrified. Now, the only thing he could do was smile. "I know you won't eat me," he said softly.

"Good. Does that mean you'll spend more time out of your bedroom?"

She was insistent, but that seemed to be a trait most dragons shared. Tim hadn't taken no for an answer when York had tried to convince him he was fine staying in his bedroom earlier, and Marcel's mother wasn't either. The clan seemed intent on dragging York out of his isolation whether he liked it or not, and he wasn't sure what to think of that.

"Why does York look terrified? Have you cornered him?" a voice asked from behind York.

York knew who it belonged to, so he didn't have to turn around to check. He hadn't expected Leo to save him, which was one more thing he didn't know what to think about.

"I didn't corner him," Marcel's mother protested. "I just wanted to talk to him. It's not easy to do when he doesn't leave his bedroom, and I don't want to bother him there."

Leo came to stand next to York, gently bumping their shoulders together. York didn't dare look up. He didn't know if Leo had done it on purpose, but he wanted to believe he had.

He shouldn't like Leo as much as he did. For one, they'd barely spent time together, which meant York didn't know the guy. Maybe Leo left his dirty socks all over the place, and maybe he didn't brush his teeth every night. Maybe York would find something he hated about the guy if he got to

11

know him, and he'd realize he needed to stay away.

But from what little York knew, he could tell Leo was a good person. He didn't have to step in to rescue York from Marcel's parents, yet here he was.

"You know you can be overwhelming," Leo gently teased Marcel's mother.

Corinne grinned, a smile too full of teeth. "Oh? Are you intimidated by me, then?" she asked, clearly teasing.

Leo laughed. "I might be if I hadn't known you since I was a child. You wouldn't hurt a fly."

"Unless that fly hurts my babies." She looked at York. "In case you're wondering, that includes you."

For a moment, York thought she was telling him he was the fly. Then, her gentle smile told him she was saying she viewed him as her child, and the pain that caused almost sent York running.

No one had loved him since Cooper died. No one had wanted to protect York because they viewed him as family and wouldn't be able to stand a world without him in it. Now, someone seemed to love him that much again, and it was Marcel's mother. How was that possible?

"You're overwhelming him again," Marcel's father said.

"Well, York and I have to go anyway," Leo declared. "We have plans."

York almost asked him what he was talking about, but he realized Leo was trying to give him an out, so instead, he nodded. He allowed Leo to gently touch his back and lead him outside after they said their goodbyes, but once they were in the hallway, he had no idea what to say or do or even if he should say or do anything. The least he could do was thank Leo, so he turned to face him, never looking up from the floor. "Thank you."

That done, he turned and started to leave.

He should have known it wouldn't be that easy.

The clan was welcoming him as if he were one of theirs, and it was as confusing as it was touching. Leo wasn't an exception to that, even though he'd been pissed with York when they'd first met. Marcel was his best friend, closer to a brother from what York had seen, and it would have destroyed him to lose Marcel.

York knew exactly how that felt. He'd lost his brother, and it had been like losing a limb or half his heart.

"No one in the clan blames you for what happened with Marcel," Leo gently said.

That was enough to get York to stop moving. He didn't look back, but he couldn't avoid hearing what Leo had to say.

"And you *are* part of this clan," Leo continued. "People have been giving you time and space to get used to everything, but if you don't give them what they want, eventually, they'll try taking it."

"I don't *understand* what they want," York whispered.

"Isn't it obvious? They want to get to know you. They want to see that you feel at home here with us. I think many clan dragons believe you're afraid of us because you think we'll hurt you, and they don't like that. You haven't given them the opportunity to show you that's not so, but I think you should."

"I don't understand you, either," York blurted out. "I almost killed one of your clan members, yet you want me to be part of the clan. You should want me to leave as soon as possible, but instead, you gave me a room and fed me and everything. Why?"

"Because we're not like Curt. Because we understand why you did what you did, and we wish we could help you with your brother. Unfortunately, there's nothing we can do about that, but we *can* make sure you're safe and as happy as possible."

A sob escaped York's throat, and he pressed his lips

together. Leo wasn't the first person to tell him why the clan was so welcoming, but none of their explanations made it easier to understand. York wasn't sure he could.

He didn't know why Marcel and his family had forgiven him so easily. He didn't know why the clan had welcomed him with open arms even though he'd hurt one of theirs.

Maybe he didn't have to understand. Maybe it would be enough for him to take what was being offered with both hands and hold on until he felt like part of the clan.

But that wasn't how York felt right now, and as he ran back to his room, he wondered if he'd really be able to feel like he'd found the one place where he belonged.

CHAPTER TWO

Y ork stared at Victor. "I've already tried that, and it didn't work."

Victor's smile was patient. "That's kind of the point. You need to try again and again until it does."

York frowned. He understood what Victor was asking him to do, but he doubted it would make any difference. He should have known better when he'd asked Victor to help him.

He'd seen Victor train with Lindsey and even Will, and everyone had pushed him to take advantage of Victor's presence. Victor wasn't a teacher, but he had years of experience in being a psychic. Most of his family could see ghosts, which meant he'd been in that world since he was a child. He knew what he was doing, and York had hoped he'd be able to tell him how to find Cooper.

So he'd followed Victor outside when Victor went for his usual walk around the yard. Victor hadn't seemed surprised to see him, nor had he been angry. Instead, when York asked if he could help, he'd agreed. That was how they'd ended up sitting on a stone bench between the trees.

York could see the house from where he was, but that was only because the trees didn't have their leaves anymore. He suspected that once summer came back, the house would be hidden from the bench, and it would feel like a haven. Not that York needed one, but it was always nice to have a place where he knew he could be alone without dragons hunting him because they wanted to talk.

"York?"

York forced himself to smile. He didn't want Victor to think he wasn't up for this, which was what would happen if he didn't start working harder. "All right. I'll try again."

Victor slowly nodded. "You know you don't have to do this, right?"

"How else am I going to find my brother?"

Victor hesitated.

York already knew what Victor wanted to tell him, and he understood. It wasn't healthy for him to focus so much on getting his brother back, since Cooper was dead, and even if they could see each other again, that would never change.

York didn't care. Cooper had been his only family for a long time, and even before their parents died, they'd been close. When Cooper died, York had lost the last part of his family, and he wanted it back, even if he could never touch Cooper again. It would be enough for him to know that Cooper was all right and that he wasn't gone from the world entirely. It was probably selfish, but Cooper would understand.

York was sure of it.

The stone bench was cold and hard under his butt, but he focused on his brother instead of that. He thought of Cooper, of the sound he made when he laughed, of how it had felt to be hugged by him and protected. Once he had Cooper's image firmly in place, York pulled with his mind. He kept repeating Cooper's name to himself, probably whispering it out loud but not caring about it. He'd make a fool of himself any day if it meant getting Cooper back.

But when York opened his eyes, Cooper was nowhere to be seen.

"It's all right," Victor said gently. "It takes a lot of time to understand how to do this. Once it clicks, it'll be easier to pull your brother or any other ghost to you."

York shot to his feet and started pacing. "How can I not do this? I'm a psychic. I should be able to do it without having to ask for help."

"You're pushing yourself too much. You might be a psychic, but you were never trained. You can't pretend to know how to do all of this right away. I promise you that soon enough, you'll be able to do it without even thinking about it."

York didn't want to fight with Victor, but he was frustrated. "When? I've been working on this forever. Even before I met you, I tried to pull Cooper to me, but I was never able to."

"You lost your brother, then went through everything with Curt, so I'm not surprised you're having trouble. You're demanding too much of yourself, even though you don't want to accept that. You need to give yourself time to heal from what happened and realize you truly are safe. Have you ever thought that maybe you can't pull your brother to you because you're not sure it would be safe for you to?"

York snorted. "Why wouldn't it be safe?"

"Curt would have used your brother. Maybe you didn't want that to happen."

"Of course I don't want it to happen, but I'm not with Curt anymore. I should be able to do it now."

"You will be."

But it wasn't enough. York needed more. He needed his brother, but he was unable to pull Cooper to himself. What good was he as a psychic if he couldn't even do this? He could have asked Victor to do it for him, but what about when Victor wasn't around? York needed to get this right.

He shook his head and stepped away. Victor frowned and started getting to his feet, but York couldn't face him. "I'll go back to my room," he said.

"You don't have to. We can try again."

"I'm sure you have better things to do with your time. I'm sorry for wasting it."

York turned around, ignored Victor calling for him, and rushed back toward the house. Victor was trying to help, and York was grateful, but it didn't change anything. He felt he was taking advantage of the clan already, and it wouldn't get better if he was taking advantage of Victor, too.

And he was. No matter how frustrated York was, Victor was a good teacher. He was patient and tried to make York see he needed more time, but York couldn't afford to take that time. As soon as he had Cooper back, he'd leave the clan, and while he wasn't looking forward to it, he knew it was the right thing to do. The clan had done too much for him, considering what he'd done to them, and he was done feeling guilty. Hopefully, leaving the dragons behind would help with that.

York wasn't sure what he'd do otherwise.

York should go back to his room, but he was starting to feel caged in, even though it was by his own hand. Instead of heading back inside the house, he walked around the yard for a bit longer, hoping it would be enough to calm himself. By the time he got back to the stone bench, it was empty, and there were no signs of Victor. York hoped he hadn't offended him, but he wasn't sure he'd have the courage to ask Victor if he had. Maybe he could show Victor that he'd listened to his lessons?

York sat on the bench, deciding to try to call his brother to him again. He sat cross-legged, ignored the cold, and thought of Cooper and what they could do once they were reunited. It was all a dream, but York could imagine them traveling. Cooper wouldn't have to pay for plane tickets or anything like that, so they could spend time exploring the places they promised they'd visit together. York imagined them on a beach somewhere, maybe under palm trees. It would be warm, and York could almost feel the sand under his feet. He found himself smiling, and when he opened his eyes, he was sure Cooper would be standing in front of him.

He wasn't.

York blinked at the empty yard in front of him. This time, he couldn't stop the tears and didn't even try. He was alone and could give in to the sadness that wrapped around his heart like an iron fist.

He was alone in the world. His brother was dead, and York was never getting him back. What was he supposed to do with his life now? How was he supposed to go on without Cooper?

"York?"

York startled so hard he almost fell off the bench. He quickly reached up to dry his tears, then plastered a fake smile on his lips and turned to look at Leo. "I promise I wasn't doing anything bad."

Leo stood there, wearing an old pair of jeans with holes in the knees and a dark sweater that had seen better days. York was ready to bet that if he buried his nose against Leo's neck, Leo would smell like the outside on a cold fall day. He was tempted to try, just to see if he was right.

Leo was still staring. "I never said you were doing something bad."

"Good, because I really wasn't. I should go. I'm sure you need to clean the bench or something like that." York's eyes widened. "Not that I'm saying it's the only thing you're good at. I'll clean the bench if you need me to. I'm the one who used it, after all."

Why did Leo fluster York so much? Maybe it was because of what had just happened with Victor, but York felt like he was about to start crying again, and he'd rather die than do so in front of Leo. Leo was a strong man, and he didn't look like the kind of person who cried and hid in a yard away from people. He had his life in hand and knew what he was doing, which was something York wasn't sure he could ever achieve.

And, damn, if that thought didn't make him want to start crying again.

Leo could see York was about to run away. He'd noticed York and Victor training earlier, and he hadn't been surprised when York had left Victor behind. He'd been running then, too, but Leo didn't want York to run away from him. He wasn't quite sure how to avoid that, but he raised his hands as if dealing with a spooked horse.

"It's fine," he promised. "I'm not offended. It *is* my job to clean up the yard, including that bench."

York tried getting up, but his feet tangled together, and he almost flopped on his face instead. Leo lunged forward, narrowly managing to grab York's arm and push him back into a sitting position.

York's cheeks were so red his face looked like it was about to explode. "I'm sorry about this," York said, avoiding looking at Leo. "I'm not usually so clumsy."

"Aren't you?"

To Leo's surprise, York laughed. "Okay, maybe I am. I hate that I'm clumsy in front of you, though."

Leo sat next to York on the bench. He didn't want to scare him, but it felt like York might be about to open up, and he didn't want to miss this opportunity. It felt like it might never happen again.

Leo didn't know if York was afraid of him because he was a dragon shifter or because he was Marcel's best friend. It was possible it was a mix of the two, along with the fact that Leo had been angry at him for a long time for what had happened to Marcel. He'd never have the opportunity to apologize if York didn't give him a chance to do so, though. Maybe today, York felt good enough to spend just a little time with him.

"I didn't treat you the way I should have," Leo said.

York turned wide, damp eyes at him. "What are you talking about? Everyone has been nice to me, even though I feel I don't deserve it."

"You do deserve it. Someone took advantage of how young you are and of the fact that you lost your brother and were desperate to get him back. I'm not saying that what you did was right, but I understand why you did it. If I'd had to do something like that to save Marcel, I might have done it, too."

York shook his head, and his too-long hair moved around his face. Leo wanted to reach out and tuck the strands behind York's ears, but he didn't dare.

"You'd never have done what I did," York whispered.

"I think I would have. I think many people would have, including Jerome and me." They were the ones who'd been the angriest at York.

"I'm sure Jerome would have."

"Not me?"

York shrugged. "Maybe, but you don't strike me as the kind of person who would hurt someone to get what you want."

"I'd hurt someone I don't know if it meant saving the life of someone I love, though. I wouldn't be happy about it, and I might even hesitate, but if it meant saving someone I love, I'd do pretty much anything."

York nodded once. "That's how I feel, too."

Leo didn't want to push York, but he was curious. "You're still looking for Cooper?"

York glanced away as if embarrassed. "I don't think I'll ever stop."

"That's understandable. He was your only family for a long time, wasn't he?"

"Yeah. I can't imagine a life without him."

Even though he was already living it. Leo could only

imagine how hard all of this had been on York. "How can you be sure Cooper is still around?"

"I'm not."

"But you get angry at yourself when you can't pull him to you. What if he moved on? You can try calling him to you for the rest of your life, but he'll never come. What will you do then? Will you keep on getting angry and pushing everyone away?"

York was staring down at his hands now. "I don't know. I can't imagine living so long without my brother. Maybe it makes me an idiot, but I'm not going to stop trying to get Cooper back. Without him, I don't have anyone, and I can't stand life on my own."

Leo frowned. "But that's not true."

"What's not true?"

"That you don't have anyone without your brother. I know you don't feel at home here yet, but you will eventually. We're your family now. You don't have to be close to every single clan member, but surely you and Tim have become friends. I've seen you two around together." And Leo knew that if York gave Marcel a chance, they'd become friends, too. Marcel was worried about York, and Leo hadn't fully understood why until recently.

"I know the clan means well, but I don't know if I can accept everything you're offering. I don't feel like I deserve it after what I did."

"Look, if Marcel doesn't hold that against you, then you shouldn't, either. He's fine. He wants to be your friend. If you want to do something good, do that for him."

"I guess I don't understand why he'd want to be my friend after what I did to him."

"Do you *have* to understand it?"

"What do you mean?"

"This is Marcel's choice. The two of you have been through

something I can only imagine, and he wants to be there for you, even though you don't seem to understand why. I don't think you have to, though. I get that you're not used to having people on your side, but the clan and Marcel are. If you just give us a chance, we can show you that. We can show you that you're not alone, even without Cooper." Leo was afraid that if they didn't manage to do that, York would continue blaming himself both for Marcel's situation and for not being able to get his brother back.

"I just don't understand."

York sounded desperate to wrap his mind around the fact that the clan wanted him, but Leo didn't know how to make him see that it was true. "Would it be okay even if you didn't? Do you think you can accept the fact that you're part of the clan and that we want you with us even without knowing why we feel that way?"

"I don't know. If I was in your place, I'd have kicked myself out long ago. Hell, I wouldn't even have welcomed me, to begin with. I don't get how hurting one of you can result in me getting everything I've ever wanted in life."

York's wide eyes told Leo he probably hadn't meant to say that out loud.

Tough shit. He had, and now that Leo knew, he'd try to convince him that whatever had happened in his past, he deserved to be happy and, like he'd said, to get everything he'd ever wanted in life.

York hadn't meant to blurt that out, but it was too late to take back his words. He got to his feet, ready to leave before making an even worse fool of himself, but Leo stopped him with a hand on his arm. He didn't touch York for long, just enough for York to stop moving.

"No one blames you for what happened," Leo said.

He sounded convinced, and York wondered how long it would take him to believe the people telling him that. Leo wasn't the first. Marcel had told York he didn't blame him for what he'd done, as had Marcel's parents. Elijah had told York he wouldn't have welcomed him in the clan if he hadn't been sure York was a good person.

And still, York couldn't believe them. He didn't understand how they felt this way when he would never forgive someone who'd done what he'd done.

Where did that leave him? Would he ever be able to accept the fact that these people didn't see him the way he saw himself, or would he keep on wondering when they'd eventually change their minds and decide that kicking him out was for the best?

He didn't want to feel this way. He didn't want to believe he was a bad person and that he didn't deserve any of this. He *wanted* to believe Leo and everyone else, to settle down and finally find out if he could live a life without his brother.

But no matter what everyone said, York wasn't sure they truly didn't blame him. If he hadn't forgiven himself, how could they have? How could they see beyond his actions when he couldn't? What if they were trying to do the right thing but were unable to do it?

York couldn't allow himself to rely on the clan when they might kick him out the next time something happened. He wasn't planning on allying with Curt again, but he wasn't perfect. He might do something the clan didn't approve of, and then he'd be ruined because he'd be alone again, and he didn't know if he could survive it a second time.

It was better for him not to come to rely on the clan any more than he already was. Maybe it was time for him to leave, although he couldn't imagine what he'd do. He'd have to live on the streets, since he didn't have an income. He could find a job, but what could he do? He might have to leave this town if he didn't want to cross paths with Curt or the clan again. The thought of being that alone and of what his life would be was enough to make him want to start crying again.

Besides, there was Cooper to think of. If York wanted his brother back, he couldn't do it on his own. He couldn't even pull Cooper to him, for fuck's sake. What did he think he'd be able to do if he were on his own?

There was also the fact that he owed it to the clan and Marcel to get rid of Curt. He couldn't do it alone, but the clan was willing to let York help. There wasn't much he could do, especially since he didn't have more information to give them, but he'd try. That was the main reason he was still here, and while it was a relief not to sleep in the street, it wouldn't last forever. He should probably make the most of it.

Or maybe not. Maybe making the most of it would be taking advantage of the clan, and that was the last thing he wanted to do.

All in all, York was freaking confused and didn't know how to deal with any of this.

He stepped away from the bench, thankful when Leo didn't try to stop him again. "I appreciate what you're trying to do," he said slowly. "You and everyone in the clan are good people. Maybe too good, because someone could take advantage of you."

"Is that what you think you're doing?" Leo didn't sound like he blamed York but rather like he was curious.

York swallowed. "Isn't it obvious that it's what I'm doing? I don't deserve any of this."

Leo frowned. "I'm not sure how to get you to believe me when I say that everyone here agrees you belong here. You didn't have the best start in life, and many clan members know what that's like. The clan gave them a chance, and they want to do the same for you. You need to stop punishing yourself for what happened with Marcel. No one says it wasn't the wrong thing to do, but in the end, no one was hurt, and you did it because you were forced to."

"I just wanted Cooper back."

"And no one blames you for that. We all know that's not why you stayed, though. You're not that kind of person. Once you realized you wouldn't get your brother back, you would have left if you could have. You certainly wouldn't have helped Curt with Marcel if you'd had a choice. He forced you to hurt Marcel, and even through that, you took care of Marcel to the best of your ability considering the circumstances. You tried helping him, and it's not something we'll ever forget. I understand it's not easy for you to wrap your mind around what has been happening and to accept that we want you here, but I don't think you'll settle down until you do that. Give us a chance, York. We gave you one, and I feel it's the least we deserve from you."

He was right. The problem was that York had no idea how to believe him and the others. He hated himself and didn't understand why they didn't, too.

He turned and walked away, and Leo let him this time. Even though York didn't think he'd ever be able to believe Leo, Marcel, and everyone else, he couldn't stop thinking about it.

Could the clan be his home permanently? Had he found the family he'd yearned for since he'd lost Cooper?

Or was he only trying to fool himself in the attempt to cling to this life he didn't deserve?

CHAPTER THREE

York swallowed. No matter what everyone said, York didn't have much time. Eventually, he'd leave the clan behind, but before doing that, he needed to find his brother.

The last training session with Victor had been a disaster, but York wasn't giving up. He couldn't, when Cooper had always been the most important person in his life. Even though he was dead, that hadn't changed, and York wasn't giving up on finding his brother. He didn't care what others thought of his obsession. He couldn't afford to.

But he couldn't do this on his own. Even with Victor's help, he wasn't sure he'd be able to do it. He *definitely* wouldn't be able to if he was on his own, though, so he was ready to grovel and beg so Victor would agree to continue helping him.

He wasn't exactly looking forward to it.

He swallowed and stared at the door in front of him. Victor, along with his brothers, Marcel, and a bunch of other people, had moved in with the clan. Everyone had agreed it was safer, considering Curt was still out there and pissed at them, but even with so many more people in the house, it didn't feel crowded. That was how big it was, and York still had trouble wrapping his mind around it. It was one more reason to stick to his room. At least there, he wouldn't get lost.

But he couldn't stay in his room if he wanted to do this, and he couldn't hover in the hallway, staring at a closed door. If he wanted his brother back, he needed to take the first step.

He felt like that was what he always did. He took a step forward, then ended up being pushed backward. It was a constant fight to move on, and he was so freaking tired.

He raised a hand and knocked on the door. For a moment, everything was silent. Then, a man laughed, and the sound of footsteps made York want to run away. Instead, he stood his ground, trying to smile as the door opened.

Tim's eyes widened when he saw York, and he beamed. "York. What are you doing out of your bedroom? Not that I'm not happy to see you because I am, but I'm surprised. You don't usually leave your room."

York felt his cheeks flush. He looked away, even though he'd started considering Tim a friend. Tim wouldn't have it otherwise, and it was good to have someone to talk to.

"Don't be rude," Victor gently chided. "And let the man in. He's here for a reason, isn't he?"

When York walked into the room, he realized what Tim and Victor had been doing and instantly wished he'd waited a bit longer to knock. Tim's shirt was buttoned all wrong, and Victor's cheeks were red and his hair was all over the place.

York stared down at his feet. "I apologize for bothering you."

"You're not bothering us," Victor assured him. "Do you want to sit down?"

"I need to talk to you." York might as well get it out of the way. "About my brother. I want to try again."

Victor didn't look surprised. "Of course. Do you want to do it now?"

York hadn't expected the offer, but he nodded. "That would be great."

"I guess that means I'm leaving," Tim said. He was still smiling, and he moved toward Victor.

"I can come back later if the two of you are busy," York quickly said.

"It's fine," Victor assured him. "Besides, Tim has work to do. His cousin won't be happy if he doesn't start soon."

Tim grimaced. "You really had to remind me of Jerome?"

"We both know you're still trying to impress him. Do you want all the work you've done to be for nothing? Because he's only waiting for you to take a wrong step."

Tim scowled. "Sometimes, I hate him."

Victor patted Tim's chest. "You don't. Besides, I'm pretty sure he's just teasing you. He trusts you, and he offered you a job. He knows how good you are."

Tim was still grumbling when he left the room.

York understood how he felt. Jerome didn't trust York, and he made sure York knew it every time they were in the same room. York didn't blame him after what he'd done to Marcel, who was Jerome's brother. He'd be pissed, too, if someone had hurt Cooper.

Someone *had* hurt Cooper. The reminder made York want to scream, but instead, he focused on Victor.

Victor gestured at the small sitting area by the windows. "Why don't we sit down?"

York nodded and followed Victor's lead. At least this time, his ass didn't feel like it was about to fall off. The couch was much more comfortable than the stone bench outside, and York wasn't cold.

"Have you tried calling your brother on your own since the last time we spoke?" Victor asked.

York hesitated, then nodded. "It didn't work."

"I'm sorry to hear that. It's good that you trained, though."

"Is it? Because it feels that nothing I do is making a difference." York sucked in a breath. "I just want my brother back. I know most people don't have the opportunity to do anything like that, but I do. What good am I as a psychic if I can't even see my brother?"

"I'm not here to tell you whether I think what you're doing is wrong or right. That's something you have to decide, but I do hope you'll manage to talk to your brother again eventually. You need closure, and you clearly haven't had it. If there's one good thing about being a psychic, it's that you have the opportunity to do this."

"But I can't. I can't find my brother, and I can't pull him to me."

Victor slowly nodded. "Have you thought that maybe, it has more to do with the rest of your life than it does with your psychic abilities?"

"What do you mean?"

"Well, there have been many changes in your life recently. You're not stuck with Curt anymore, and you found a home and a family. You've been welcomed into the clan. You've met many new people, and it's obvious you're having trouble dealing with everything. Maybe your psychic abilities have taken a step back to give you the opportunity to wrap your mind around everything and get used to it."

York frowned. "Are you having problems, too?"

"No, but my situation is different."

That much was right. "You've been trying to help the clan from the start, while I tried hurting a clan member."

"That's not what I meant. It's different because I'm older and have more experience, and I have a family. Living with so many people is strange, but I grew up with three brothers and my parents. Besides, I also have Tim. His presence by my side is soothing, and while I'm overwhelmed, I know I can always turn to him. I'm not sure you have that."

York shrugged. "I don't need it. I just need to talk to my brother."

Victor stared at him. "How about we try working on this from a different angle?"

York wasn't sure he liked the sound of that. "What kind of angle?"

"It's clear you still feel guilty about what you did to Marcel. You expect the clan to hurt you or, at the very least, to kick you out. How about you try to find something to do for the clan? Maybe helping them would help you feel more relaxed and like you belong, and I think it would unlock your abilities. You want to talk to your brother, but something is clearly stopping you from doing it."

"I'm not doing it on purpose," York snapped.

"I never thought you were. But maybe your subconscious knows that once you manage to talk to your brother, you'll leave, and that wouldn't be the best thing for you."

York had to look away. How did Victor know he was planning to leave? "What do you think I should do?" he asked.

"I don't know. Nothing stupid or dangerous. But you've been keeping to yourself, so maybe spending more time with clan members and helping around the house would change things. You don't have to become the life of the party, just to let people in. Why don't we go outside? You don't have to talk to anyone, but it would be good if people saw you."

York thought of Leo, who'd already tried helping him. He doubted he could do anything like what Victor was saying, but there had to be other ways to help the clan. Maybe he could try reaching out to Curt and find out where he was. He could tell Curt the dragons had taken him and that he needed help. Curt wouldn't come for him, but he might tell him where to find him. That was what the clan wanted. Then, once the clan had gotten rid of Curt, York would truly be free of him, and he could focus on finding Cooper.

It didn't sound like the best of plans, but it was the only one York could come up with.

Leo had a plan. He wasn't sure it was a good one, but that wouldn't stop him from putting it in motion.

For whatever reason, he was drawn to York. He wanted to help the other man and show him he was a clan member, that he was home and didn't have to keep running. It wouldn't be easy to do if York stuck to his rooms, so Leo had decided to take him out.

The easiest way to convince York that people cared about him was to show him. Spending more time out of the room would help, as would having York talk to people. It would be overwhelming, but Leo wasn't planning on throwing him in the middle of the clan's Christmas party. He'd be there every step of the way, and they'd start small.

He looked around. He'd lived here his entire life, so having many people around him, talking, laughing, and sharing living spaces, was normal. The noise level was, too, but he could see how overwhelming it could be to someone who wasn't used to it. York only had his brother after their parents had passed away, and that wasn't a lot of people.

Operation *convince York he was home* had officially started.

Leo extricated himself from his favorite armchair in the living room and stretched. He'd been warm and cozy next to the fireplace, and he felt instantly colder, but he had things to do, and he wouldn't be able to do them by staying here.

The first thing on his to-do list was to find York. It would be easier to convince him he belonged if he was actually there. So, Leo left the living room and headed upstairs to York's bedroom. That was where York could usually be found, no matter the time of day.

It was good that York felt safe in his bedroom. The problem was that the few times Leo had seen it, the room hadn't changed from before York moved into it. It still looked like a normal, boring guest room, with no personal touches except for a picture of York and his brother on the nightstand.

Or at least, he assumed the guy in the picture with York was his brother. He hadn't asked and wasn't sure York would tell him if he did. York and the guy in the picture looked like each other enough that Leo didn't have many doubts the man was Cooper.

He'd been handsome, almost as handsome as York. In the picture, there was a weariness to him, as if he was exhausted, and from what little Leo knew, he suspected that was true. But no matter how tired Cooper had been, he'd still been beaming at the camera, his arm wrapped around a younger York's shoulders. York had been looking up at his brother instead of the camera, and his love for Cooper shone in his gaze. Leo understood why it was so important to York to get his brother back, even though Cooper was dead. Leo wasn't sure York would ever get Cooper back, but there was nothing he could do to help York in that situation. That meant he was planning on focusing on everything else.

But York wasn't in his bedroom.

For a moment, Leo was nonplussed when no one opened the door. He was used to finding York here when he visited, but it wasn't like York was a prisoner in his bedroom. He had free reign of the house and the yard as much as anyone else, and he could visit his friends. He might be with one of them, but Leo suspected he wouldn't find York inside the house.

So he headed outside.

He went to the stone bench where he and York had talked not long ago. He'd wanted to help York back then, too, but he hadn't been sure how to do it. He still wasn't, but he was willing to give it a try anyway.

He heard the voices before he saw the two men sitting on the bench. York and Victor were softly talking, and from the sound of it, Victor was giving York instructions. Leo hesitated, not wanting to bother or interrupt them if it was a lesson, but before he could decide whether or not he should go back to the house, he put his foot down on a branch. Its crack was loud, almost like a gunshot, and there was no way Victor and York hadn't heard it.

Leo cleared his throat and stopped trying to be quiet.

"York?" he called out.

There was a moment of silence before York answered. "Leo?"

Leo grinned. "Yep."

Now that he was closer, he could see Victor leaning closer to York, whispering something that made York blush fiercely. Victor turned to Leo, grinning at him, and Leo wondered if the two had been talking about him.

The thought of that possibility shouldn't send flutters through his stomach, but it did. Whatever York was doing to him, it was pulling him deeper into York's net, and Leo couldn't find it in himself to resist.

He didn't want to.

"I was just going back inside," Victor said as he got to his feet.

"But I haven't gotten Cooper yet," York protested.

Victor put a hand on his shoulder and squeezed. "Remember what we talked about. You feel guilty, and like you don't belong here, like it's not your place. Try thinking about something you could do for the clan. They don't *need* you to do anything, but I believe it would make you feel more like you belong, which in turn will mean you're more relaxed."

York frowned. "And being more relaxed would make it easier to focus my abilities on Cooper and pull him to me."

"Exactly."

York shook his head. "I don't understand how you think this will work."

"You don't have to understand. Just try, and next time we see each other, you can tell me what happened. Continue focusing on your brother and trying to pull him to you. Eventually, you'll manage, even without my help. But you need more than the obsession with getting your brother back. I'm sure he would have wanted you to build a life and be happy, and maybe that's why you can't get him to come to you."

York's eyes widened. "You think he's angry at me?"

"I have no idea how he feels or if he's even still around. But think about it. When you finally get him back, what will he think of your life here?"

With that, Victor seemed to be done talking. He walked past Leo, winking at him as he did so. Leo had no idea what it meant, but he felt like Victor knew how he felt about York.

The entire clan probably did.

Leo had never been discreet when he felt strongly about someone. Until now, he'd been lucky that, usually, his feelings were shared. There was no way to know how York felt about him, but he'd seemed receptive enough when they'd talked the last time they were at the bench. Hopefully, York would give Leo the time of day. Leo would have to come up with an alternative if that wasn't the case.

"Did you need anything?" York asked when Leo moved closer.

"I was looking for you."

York frowned. "Why? Has something happened?"

Leo shook his head. "You need to stop thinking of the worse possibilities every time someone talks to you. No, nothing has happened. I just thought we could do something together."

York frowned. "What do you mean?"

Leo decided to take a chance. He reached out, offering York his hand. "Do you trust me?"

Did York trust Leo?

York's first instinct was to say no, but he pressed his lips together and really thought about it.

Leo hadn't done anything to cause York not to trust him. He'd been wary of York in the beginning, but that made sense, considering what York had done to his best friend. As soon as

Marcel had shown he didn't hold a grudge, Leo had relaxed, unlike Jerome. He'd been nice to York, talked to him often, and even made a point of looking for him when York felt like hiding.

York looked at the man standing in front of him. "I do," he said. His heart raced as he realized it was true. He did trust Leo, and whatever Leo had in mind, York would follow him through it. He was actually kind of excited, and he couldn't wait to find out what would happen next.

It had been a long time since he felt that way. Even when Cooper was still part of York's life, things hadn't been easy. Cooper had worked several jobs just to keep a roof over their heads and food in York's stomach, and York would always be grateful for that. He'd had enough then, with just his brother, and he felt guilty now, realizing that maybe he needed more.

Leo grinned and took York's hand. "Let's go, then."

York could only follow when Leo pulled him along. "Where are we going?"

"Do you really want to know, or do you want it to be a surprise?"

"What kind of surprise? A good one?"

"I guess surprises aren't always good. I do think it's a good one, though. I'm taking you shopping."

York had no idea what he was talking about. "I don't need to go shopping."

"You only have a few pairs of jeans and three or four sweaters. You need more clothes, but that's not what I was thinking about."

"What, then?" The thought of going shopping with Leo made York anxious but also happy. He wanted to spend more time alone with Leo, even though it was probably a bad idea.

"The few times I've seen your bedroom, it was just like before. You don't have any personal items except for the picture on your nightstand, and I suspect it's not helping you make

36

you feel like you're part of the clan. The state of your bedroom shows you're still a visitor, and that's not what you are."

"I don't need anything else, though. I don't want to be a bother."

York had no doubt that Elijah, the clan leader, wouldn't have a problem with any of this, even if the clan had to pay for it. He'd told York several times that now that he was a clan member, the clan would be taking care of him. It felt odd, though. York was used to working, but getting a job in town would be too dangerous. It would be too easy for Curt to find him, which was why Elijah had asked him to wait to try finding something. That made York uncomfortable, because he owed Elijah and the clan everything, and he hated taking advantage of them more than he already had.

"York?" Leon asked.

York blinked at him. Leo had slowed down, but they were still outside, with the house in the distance. Leo's smile had started to slip, and while York wanted it back, he needed the situation to be clear.

"I don't need anything," he insisted.

Leo shook his head, but instead of pulling York toward the house, he went sideways. York understood why when they reached a line of cars parked by the house.

"Really," he repeated. "The bedroom is more than I've had in a long time."

"And I hate that," Leo said with a tiny snarl at the end of the last word. "I saw where you lived when you and Marcel were there. No one should have to live in a place like that, and no one should have to live alone."

"Some people like living alone."

Leo looked back as he stopped next to a silver car. "Do *you* like living alone?"

"I'm fine on my own."

"I'm sure you are, but it's not what I asked. Do you enjoy

living alone?"

York didn't know how to answer that. Before, he'd lived with his family and his brother. Then, after his parents died, Cooper had always been there for him. Even after Cooper had died, York hadn't been alone for long because Curt had found him. He'd shared living spaces with other psychics, and while they hadn't been a family, it helped him not feel alone.

And now, he had the dragons.

"I'm fine either way," he murmured.

Leo snorted, opened the passenger door of his car, and gently pushed York toward it. "That's not what I asked, but fine. Let's act as if you answered and told me you don't like living on your own."

York laughed. "That's not what I said."

"No one likes being on their own, at least not for long. I understand some people are introverts and need time alone to recharge, but everyone needs a family, be it the family you grew up with or a chosen one."

And the dragons had decided to be York's chosen family.

York still had no idea why, but he was starting to understand that no matter how hard he tried to convince himself that he'd be able to leave them behind, it wouldn't be as easy as he was pretending. It wasn't just because of the clan in general, but also because of people like Tim, Victor and Leo, people York wasn't sure he *could* leave.

Leo closed the passenger door and quickly walked around the car.

York couldn't deny that the thought of making his bedroom more his was tempting, but he truly didn't want to be a bother.

Once Leo was in the car, York turned to him. "I don't have any money."

"You won't need to pay for it."

"It wouldn't be right to have the clan pay for all of this,

though. You've already given me a home. It's more than enough."

"I don't believe it is, but if you don't want the clan to pay, then I will."

"I don't see how that's any better."

"Don't you want to make me happy?"

Leo had York there. "Maybe. I just don't see how buying *me* stuff would make *you* happy."

"I like taking care of people. Most of my friends don't need me to, especially since they found love. It would be a favor you do for me if you allowed me to do this."

York wasn't an idiot. He suspected Leo was saying a lot of not-entirely-true things just to make him say yes, but he found himself going along with it. It didn't matter if Leo truly wanted to take care of York or if he was just saying it because he wanted York to say yes. York wanted someone to take care of him, and really, who better than Leo?

"Where are we going, then?" he asked.

Leo beamed. "I know you don't want to spend a lot of money, so I have the perfect place."

That was all he said, no matter how many times York asked him for more information. He was both relieved and a bit anxious when Leo finally parked his car in front of a big store in the form of a blue box. The yellow writing told him the store's name, and while he'd never been here, he'd heard of it — and of the meatballs the restaurant sold.

"I don't know any Swedish," he warned as they left the car.

Leo laughed. "I don't think we need to know Swedish. Instead, how good are you with directions? Would you get lost in a labyrinth?"

York looked up at the store. His heart felt full in a way it hadn't in a long time. He might not understand Leo, but did it really matter? He didn't *have* to understand him.

He stepped closer, and when Leo grinned at him, he leaned

forward. Leo's eyes widened when York pressed their lips together, but York stepped back before Leo could do anything, be it kiss him or push him away.

He didn't know what had gotten into him, but he was flustered and not ready to face what he'd just done. So, instead, he started walking toward the store.

When he realized Leo was still standing there, staring at him, he looked back over his shoulder. "That shopping isn't going to do itself."

That jostled Leo out of his thoughts, and he rushed to get to York's side. Thankfully, he didn't bring up the kiss. York knew he wouldn't be able to avoid talking about it forever, but for now, he was perfectly happy to eat meatballs and make fun of the Swedish names of the furniture.

Chapter Four

L eo hadn't been able to stop thinking about the kiss. He and York hadn't talked about it, and the rest of the day had been lovely. They'd wandered in the store, trying every couch and bed they could find. A few times, it had felt as if they were shopping for their own home, and Leo was surprised at how much he wanted that. He and York had only shared a kiss, for fuck's sake. How was it possible that Leo felt so strongly about him?

But he did, and he couldn't deny it. He wanted something to happen with York, and considering the kiss, he thought York wanted the same.

But he wasn't surprised York had put space between them since then. That day had been a lot, considering York usually kept to himself, even though he'd seemed to enjoy it. They'd had lunch at the store, and after buying new sheets, lamps, rugs, and a few knickknacks, they'd headed home. Leo had helped York take everything upstairs, but York hadn't asked him to stay and help him put everything together. Leo had respected that and had left York alone, but it had been several days now, and York hadn't reached out to him.

Why? Was he confused about the kiss and how Leo had responded to it? Or was he hiding because he thought he'd made a mistake and didn't want Leo to have false hope? Or maybe he thought he'd done the wrong thing. Another possibility was that he'd been trying to gain something by kissing Leo, although Leo couldn't think of what that something could have been. Kissing him didn't give York anything more than what he already had.

Leo wouldn't know until he talked to York, but that was nearly impossible when York didn't leave his bedroom. Leo didn't want to corner him there because it was the place where he felt safest, but eventually, he might have to.

Leo had a plan for this, too. With York hiding in his room again, Tim had been bringing him meals. Some people thought Tim was coddling York, but at least this way, York was eating. Leo suspected that without Tim, York would rather not eat at all than leave his bedroom. He was good at avoiding people, even to his own detriment.

So there was only one way for Leo to get to York, and that was by taking Tim's place. When he went to dinner that evening, he gobbled down his food in minutes, keeping an eye on Tim. Tim was sitting with Victor and Victor's brothers at a table not far from Leo's, and all of them were talking and laughing. It looked like Victor and his brothers had always been part of the clan, and it was good to see.

Everyone in the clan was happy to have so many new people around. When it came to clan members, they'd never cared about what kind of shifter someone was or even if someone was a shifter at all. There weren't that many dragons left, and it felt good to have more people become part of the clan. They brought something no dragon could bring to the table, and it was nice to see. It was also nice that Tim, along with Marcel and Jerome, had found someone to love them.

And it made Leo want to find the same.

He quickly swallowed his last bite when he saw Tim getting to his feet. When Tim headed back toward the tables that held the food, Leo knew he'd fill a plate for York. He followed him, cleaning his plate and leaving it with the others as he hovered close by. He thought he'd been discreet, but he should have known better because Tim turned to him after grabbing a plate and placing it, a bottle of water, and a piece of bread on a tray. "Why are you hovering behind me?"

Leo rubbed the back of his neck. "I'm sorry. I didn't mean to make you uncomfortable."

"You didn't, but it's a bit odd. So, what can I do for you?"

"I need to talk to York."

"And he's not opening his bedroom door for you."

"I tried talking to him a few times, but he told me every-thing was fine and to go."

"Maybe that's what you should do."

"I'll leave him alone after this, but I need to talk to him first."

Tim stared at Leo for a moment. Leo had no idea what he was thinking, but he hoped Tim knew him well enough to re-alize he didn't mean any harm to York. He just wanted to talk to him.

Eventually, Tim nodded. "York's been better since he started spending time with you. I don't know what you did to spook him, but I hope he'll get over it." He held up the tray. "There. And if he yells at you, just tell him I was busy."

Leo grabbed the tray and smiled. "I doubt he'll yell at me. He's not the yelling kind of guy."

"No, but we've become friends, and he relies on me. I don't like feeling like I'm betraying him."

"I promise I mean him no harm. Something happened when we went out the other day, and it's not bad, but I believe we should talk about it. He's so used to hiding himself and how he feels that I'm not sure he knows what having a real relationship with someone is like. He's floundering, and I want to help him."

Tim cocked his head. "And to get answers."

"That would be nice, too. He's so confusing."

"I don't think most people find him confusing. Maybe it has to do with how he reacts to your presence."

"Probably. Thanks for doing this, though." Leo raised the

tray so Tim would understand what he was talking about.

"Take care of him. I know some people don't like him because of what he did, but his heart has always been in the right place. Someone took advantage of him, and it's not fair to hold a grudge when he's already apologized so many times. Besides, if Marcel doesn't hold him responsible for what happened, I don't see why anyone else should."

Leo agreed, and he was sure Tim was talking about Jerome. The man could hold a grudge like no one else.

Tim wasn't done speaking. "He has nightmares, you know?"

Leo hadn't known, and he stepped closer. "About what?"

"He never goes into details, but I know they have to do both with Cooper and what happened to him and the thing with Marcel. Sometimes, he dreams that we didn't get there in time and that Marcel died. He feels responsible, even though Marcel is perfectly fine."

"They've both been through a lot."

"I agree, and I think everyone else does, too, but York still feels he's not in the right place. I wish he could see the clan wants him with us."

"I suspect it'll take time. Right now, he's focused on his brother. Maybe once he gets that out of the way, he'll see how much he means to all of us." Because if he didn't, he'd end up leaving, and Leo didn't want that to happen any more than him dead.

"I'll be nice, and I promise that what I have to talk to him about isn't bad," he said.

"It would be easy to hurt him. I don't expect you to never make him cry, but he's fragile, and his heart even more so. Take care with him."

Knowing how much Tim cared about York humbled Leo. Tim was looking out for his best friend when no one else was. The clan didn't hate York. They were curious about him and happy to have him there, but they didn't know him and didn't love him as much as Tim did. No one did, but maybe Leo could be there for York in a different way than Tim. He didn't want him and York to be friends. He wanted more, but he had no idea if York would be open to that.

He was about to find out, hopefully.

As soon as Tim knocked on the door, York scrambled to his feet. He was starving, and while he knew he could have gotten food sooner by going downstairs, he was hiding from Leo.

And from how stupid he'd been.

York had wanted to kiss Leo almost since the first day they'd met. That feeling had grown as he'd gotten to know Leo, and now that he'd actually kissed him, he couldn't stop thinking about it.

He was an idiot.

Leo could have so much better. He could be with a dragon, for one. Surely, that was what all dragons wanted.

The thought made York frown as he reached the door. Jerome, Marcel, and Tim weren't dating other dragons. They didn't seem to care that the men they loved were psychics. Maybe dragons were supposed to date psychics? That didn't make much sense, but it gave York hope he wasn't sure how to deal with.

He swung open the door, already smiling. The smile froze on his lips when, instead of Tim, he found Leo smiling back at him. "What are you doing here?" he asked.

Leo frowned, but he answered. "Tim was going to bring you food, but I asked if I could do it."

"Why?" York knew the answer, but he was still hoping to somehow get out of the conversation they should have.

Leo didn't look impressed. "Because we need to talk, and you've been avoiding me. Can I come in?"

"Would you leave if I asked you to?"

"Of course. I'd leave and give you all the time and space you need, but we both know we should talk about what happened the other day."

York sighed and stepped back to allow Leo inside. He closed the door, and when he turned to Leo, it was to see the tray was on the dresser now. The smell coming from the plate made York's stomach grumble, but he wanted to get this conversation out of the way.

Clearly, Leo wasn't in as much of a hurry as he was because he gestured at the small desk in the corner. "Sit down."

He moved the tray there while York went into the bathroom to wash his hands. When he returned to the bedroom, he saw Leo had dragged one of the armchairs from the corner by the window to the desk so he could sit next to York while he ate.

"Have you already eaten?" York asked as he sat.

"Downstairs with everyone else."

York examined the plate. There was meatloaf, along with mashed potatoes and broccoli. Tim insisted York needed vegetables, and while York wasn't convinced about broccoli yet, it didn't taste as bad as he'd expected it to. He speared a piece with the fork he'd felt next to the plate and stuffed it into his mouth before turning his attention back to Leo.

Leo was staring at him, an odd expression on his face. York felt as if Leo was trying to read him and not coming up with much, which was how he felt about Leo, so he understood the feeling.

"I wanted to apologize," he said. He felt it was best to get it out of the way right from the beginning.

But instead of accepting the apology, Leo frowned. "What are you apologizing for this time?"

York couldn't look him in the eyes as he answered, so he looked at his plate. "Kissing you. It was inappropriate. You were trying to be nice to me, to be a friend, and I almost messed that up."

"Did you want to kiss me?"

That was a stupid question. "I wouldn't have kissed you if I didn't want to. I realize it was the wrong thing to do, though. I hope you won't hold it against me."

Leo shook his head. "How could I hold it against you when I wanted to kiss you, too? You surprised me, but not in a bad way."

York couldn't believe that. "Anyway, I'm really sorry, and I promise I won't do it again. I thought it would be easier for you if I stayed away, but I should have realized you'd want to talk about what I did. Now that we have, I'm sure you have better things to do than to sit next to me and watch me eat."

Leo surged forward, cupping York's cheek and pressing their lips together. York was so shocked that he gasped, opening his mouth to Leo. He remembered too late that he probably tasted like broccoli, but Leo didn't seem to mind. He kissed York relentlessly, pushing ahead every time York hesitated. York never wanted it to end, but Leo was right.

They needed to talk.

Because York hadn't expected this, and he was confused. What did Leo want from him? York had thought Leo would be happy to get an apology for the kiss and to put everything behind them, but instead, he was kissing him.

"I lost you again," Leo muttered, his mouth still against York's lips.

"I'm sorry."

Leo chuckled as he shook his head. "Please, stop apologizing for every single thing. I know we have a lot to talk about, but I wanted to show you that I wanted to kiss you as much as you did."

York touched his lower lip. "I think I finally got that."

That got a laugh out of Leo. "Good. I'm not sure how much

clearer I could have been to make you understand. Now, why don't you continue eating? We can talk as you do, and hopefully, by the time your plate is empty, we'll have fixed things between us."

York hadn't been aware there were things to fix between them, but he was happy to go along with Leo's plan, especially since Leo seemed convinced it was the right thing to do.

"I wanted to talk about the reason you kissed me," Leo said. "Was it because you were grateful for what I was doing? Or is there more behind it? Because I can tell you that on my side, there's more. I'm always thinking about you, and I'm pretty sure I'm falling in love with you."

York dropped his fork. He was in shock and couldn't seem to make his fingers work, even when he tried to pick up the fork again.

If he'd been confused before, that was nothing next to how he felt now. He eyed Leo, trying to read the other man. Was he truly falling in love with York? It felt impossible, but York wasn't about to tell Leo he was a liar.

He didn't want it to be true.

He didn't know if he was falling in love with Leo, but he certainly wanted to kiss him some more and maybe explore what else could happen between them. Was this how Leo felt, too? Was that why he was here, asking York how he felt?

York had no idea, but he suspected he was about to find out, and it terrified him as much as it excited him.

He wanted Leo, and it seemed like maybe, Leo wanted him, too. How was he supposed to deal with that? What was he supposed to *do*?

Leo reached for the fork York didn't seem to be able to pick up and did so for him. He placed it in York's hand, waiting for him to say something.

When he'd decided to tell York he was falling in love with him, he hadn't expected York to react this way. It seemed York was frozen, staring at Leo as if he didn't understand his words.

Maybe he didn't. Leo had been honest and clear, but who knew what went on in York's mind? Leo already knew York didn't think much of himself, so maybe something he'd said had shocked York to the point where he couldn't say anything.

Had it been a mistake? Leo wasn't sure, but either way, he couldn't go back on what he'd said.

York was still staring at him, and Leo gently nudged him with his shoulder. "You should eat," he murmured.

York blinked. Leo decided to lean back in the armchair he'd moved earlier and give him time to wrap his mind around what had just happened. Leo had already had time to understand what he was feeling and to find out what he wanted to do with all of that, but York hadn't. He'd been hiding, both from Leo and himself. He couldn't continue doing so, and while Leo couldn't wait to find out what York would want, it wouldn't happen right away.

York started moving again, but more slowly. He speared a piece of broccoli with his fork and stuffed it into his mouth, chewing almost mechanically as he continued staring at Leo.

Leo chuckled and rubbed the back of his neck. "You're making me self-conscious."

York frowned and put down his fork. "Why should you be self-conscious?"

"I don't know that I should be, but you're staring at me right after I told you I'm falling in love with you. Anyone would be self-conscious."

"I'm just—I don't understand."

Leo wasn't surprised. At least York wasn't rejecting him outright, which was more than he'd hoped for. After all, he hadn't believed he'd make it past York's door. "What don't you understand?"

York looked down from Leo to his plate. "How you can feel that way."

"I'm not sure there's anything to understand. Emotions are like that. You feel them even if they make no sense."

"And loving me makes no sense?"

Leo would have hit himself if it hadn't been ridiculous. "That's not what I said. You just took me by surprise. I didn't expect to fall in love with you, especially when we haven't spent that much time together. I feel like I know so little about you. I guess I know the important things, though, and they're enough."

York frowned. "How can they be? I kidnapped and hurt your best friend. I almost killed him, and I would have if you and the others hadn't arrived to save him. I didn't hesitate to work with an asshole who wants to take over the world and squish every single person he feels isn't good enough, which is almost everyone."

Leo shook his head. York still didn't see himself clearly, but it wouldn't send Leo running. Instead, it convinced him even more than what York needed was to be shown he could be loved. No matter how many times Leo and the others told him they didn't hold what he'd done against him, York couldn't wrap his mind around it.

In time, he would.

He wouldn't be able to ignore it. Leo would make sure of that, just like he'd make sure York knew how important he was both to him and the clan.

He reached over and took one of York's hands. York startled slightly but didn't push Leo away, allowing him to link their fingers together. They were connected like this, and when Leo leaned closer to kiss York's cheek, York didn't freak out, at least not that Leo could see.

"I know all of that, but also that you're a caring man who has gone through too much loss. You're gentle and sweet, and someone more powerful than you took advantage of that. He used the pain you felt over losing your brother, but he'd have found a way to get you to do his bidding even if Cooper had still been alive. That's the kind of person Curt is. He uses people without thinking twice about it and without caring one bit about what happens to the people he's hurting."

"But I still agreed to work for him. I knew he wasn't a good man."

"Would you have kidnapped Marcel if he hadn't forced you?"

York's eyes widened, and he shook his head. "Of course not."

"What about the spell he used against Marcel? Would you have agreed to let him do it if you'd known what it would do to Marcel?"

"No. I never wanted anyone to get hurt. I just wanted Cooper back, and I never thought Curt would hurt people."

"And that's why no one holds what happened against you. We can all see how gentle you are, and we know you'd never have done any of this if you had a choice." Leo wasn't sure this would be enough. He needed more time. "Can you just give me a chance? I mean, if you feel the same way, of course. If you can't see me as anything but a friend, I'll understand, and I'll step back. I'd like to show you how much I love you, though."

York's lower lip trembled. "I wasn't sure I'd ever hear those words again."

His brother had probably been the last person to tell York he loved him, and knowing that broke Leo's heart. York should have a life full of love and people to support him.

And he did now. He had the clan, and once he allowed them in, he'd see how much he was loved. It would take time, but Leo didn't have a problem with working hard to get York to see what was under his nose.

He leaned closer. "I'll repeat them as many times as you need me to. I'm falling in love with you, York, and I don't care what happened in the past and what you did. My only goal is to make you happy, and I hope you'll let me in. I hope you'll give me a chance to show you that I'm not lying and that you can trust me."

York finally looked up and held Leo's gaze with his own. "I do trust you," he whispered.

"What do you want, then? Because you just have to say the word, and I'll step away from all of this. I'll leave you alone."

"I don't want you to leave me alone."

Leo grinned. "Then, I'll stay. Anything else?" Leo would give York the moon if that was what York asked for.

He'd just have to come up with a plan to pull it down first.

York didn't know how to answer Leo's question, or rather, he knew how to answer it but was afraid of doing so. Leo was offering York everything he could ever have wanted, but could York take it?

He still felt he was being given a chance he didn't deserve. The clan had done that when they'd welcomed him in their midst, and now Leo was offering him so much more.

Maybe too much.

York had never been in a serious relationship. He'd had boyfriends, but they'd never lasted long, and after Cooper had died, he hadn't had the patience even for those. He'd wanted to be left alone so he could focus on getting Cooper back, and while he wasn't sure he was any closer to that than he'd been before, he'd started to realize that maybe there could be more to his life than his obsession with Cooper.

He'd never give up trying to get Cooper back. He wanted

to see his brother again, tell him what he'd done, and hope-fully, get Cooper's absolution. Cooper hadn't been hurt by what York had done, but York had still done it in his name, and he wouldn't have been happy about it. York would give anything to hear Cooper yell at him again.

But this situation had nothing to do with Cooper.

York looked at Leo, who was staring at him, looking calm as if he hadn't just cracked his heart open. York wasn't sure he'd have had so much courage. He wasn't brave, nothing like Leo thought he was. He hadn't stood up to Curt when he should have, and even though he'd done his best to keep Mar-cel safe, it hadn't taken that much from him. He wasn't sure what Leo saw in him, but he also wasn't sure he could say no to what Leo was offering.

It had been a long time since York had felt loved, and while he'd been able to ignore how much he missed it, he didn't think he could anymore. Leo's words were carved in his heart and mind, and he wanted to hear them time and time again.

He also wanted Leo.

Leo was handsome, and he was a good person. Anyone would be happy to have him in their life, and York could see how lucky he was. He might not understand how Leo could fall for him, but he didn't *have* to understand it. He just had to know that was how Leo felt.

Leo was still staring, and York needed to tell him how he felt. The problem was that he had no idea how he felt. He couldn't seem to be able to put his thoughts into an order that made sense, so he decided to blurt everything out and see what Leo could make of it.

"I *really* like you," he admitted. "I don't know if it's love, but it's like nothing I've felt before. It's just hard to focus on anything that isn't getting my brother back, you know? That's been my goal for so long that I don't know how to live with-out it."

"You don't have to live without it. I'm not asking you to give up on finding your brother. I'm just asking you to give me a chance to be in your life and take care of you and love you."

Leo's hand felt good and steady, and it made York want to lean against him. York blinked, realizing he could. That was what Leo had been saying, wasn't it? He was in love with York, and he wanted to be there for him, to support him through hard times.

When York leaned forward, Leo reacted as if he knew what York wanted. He wrapped an arm around him and pulled him closer, gently kissing his temple. York snuggled against Leo's chest. His torso was twisted weirdly, and his back already ached, but he didn't care. This was everything he'd ever wanted beyond having his brother back in his life.

"Talk to me," Leo quietly said.

York snorted. "I'm not sure what to say. I'm not even sure what to think."

"Just say out loud whatever's going through your mind. We'll sort things out together."

York nodded. Could he really allow himself to have this? He didn't deserve it, but Leo didn't seem to care, and York wanted to feel the same way. He had no doubt that eventually, he'd lose all of it. It might be because he did something stupid, or maybe because Leo realized York wasn't good enough. Whatever happened, York wouldn't have this forever, so would it be such a bad thing for him to take advantage of it while he did? Leo was offering him everything he hadn't allowed himself to think about since his brother had died. York wanted nothing more than to grab it with both hands and cling to it until he was part of Leo.

York might not want to allow himself to hope that this could be his life, but he could give in, at least for now. When Leo finally came to his senses, York would take a step back, but in the meantime, he was done resisting. He was tired, and his heart ached all the time. He was glad for the clan and the friends he'd made, but most of the time, their presence didn't feel like enough. Leo was offering York to take care of him and to love him, and even though York didn't feel it was fair to Leo, he wanted to accept.

It was entirely selfish. Eventually, he'd hurt Leo, and he'd have to deal with the consequences of that. Maybe he wasn't as good person as Leo seemed to believe, because if he was, he'd leave Leo alone. But right now, he didn't care.

He tilted his head toward Leo, and when Leo leaned down, he smiled. Their lips brushed together, the kiss achingly gentle, and York's heart raced.

No matter how many times he told himself not to hope, he wasn't sure he could avoid it. He also realized that if he gave in and allowed Leo into his heart, he'd fall in love with the man. Both of them would end up hurting once this was over, but York couldn't find it in himself to care.

He'd deal with the consequences of his actions later. For now, he kissed Leo again and told himself that Leo knew what he was doing and that no matter what happened in the future, York would be the one hurting rather than Leo.

York could deal with that.

CHAPTER FIVE

Leo felt strangely bouncy, but he'd been this way since he and York had talked. As he made his way down the hallway, he wondered if York truly believed he hadn't seen right through him.

York had said all the right things. He'd done the right things, too, kissing Leo when Leo wanted it, leaning against him and allowing him to take care of him. He'd started coming out of his room more often, and while his smiles were generally reserved for Leo and the other people he cared about, he'd relaxed around the rest of the clan.

But there was still a part of York that he kept hidden. It was as if he was ashamed of that part, which was why Leo knew what it was. York still didn't believe he deserved everything happening to him, and he expected his life to change again, and not for the better.

It would.

Leo had plans, but he couldn't put them into motion until Curt was taken care of. Once the man wasn't a danger anymore, Leo would be able to show York what the rest of his life would be like, how loved he was, and how many opportunities being a clan member offered him. Maybe Leo could even help him find his brother, even though he wasn't psychic. First, though, they had to deal with the dangerous situation they were in. None of them would be able to live their life with Curt just waiting for them to take the wrong step.

But even though he knew York still wasn't sure that what they were doing together was right, there was a bounce to

Leo's step. He tried taming his feelings, but as soon as he reached the conference room where the meeting he was headed to would be held, he knew he'd failed.

Tim was standing in front of the open door, talking to one of Victor's brothers. He looked up when he heard Leo and cocked his head as he stared at him, looking endearingly like a puppy but also like he was trying to read Leo.

Leo smiled, hoping to show him everything was fine, but from the way Tim's eyes widened, he was pretty sure he'd exaggerated.

Dammit.

"What happened to you?" Tim asked once Leo reached him and Donahue.

"Nothing. Is everyone here?" What Leo was actually asking was if York was there. Leo had offered to pick him up at his room, but York had declined because he'd been training with Victor. Leo had been tempted to ask how that was going, but it was a touchy subject for York, and Leo was unwilling to rock the boat, at least for now.

"We're still waiting for Elijah and Gunter, but they'll be here soon."

He hadn't mentioned York, so Leo hoped he was already inside. He stepped into the conference room, looking around. For a moment, he thought York had decided not to come. It would be his right, especially since he had no additional information about Curt and his people. He never said much during the meetings, and no one would have blamed him if he'd avoided them.

"There," Tim whispered, tilting his chin toward a corner of the room.

Leo understood why he hadn't spotted York right away. He wasn't sitting at the table like most people in the room. Instead, he'd chosen one of the chairs that lined the walls and was almost hiding in a plant. It was taller than him on the chair, and while Leo wasn't surprised that was where York had decided to sit, he wished York was more comfortable with the clan.

There was nothing he could do to help York feel better about himself and the clan beyond what he was already doing, but he could try.

He quickly made his way toward York just as Elijah and Gunter walked into the room. York noticed them, too, and he seemed to shrink in on himself. He hid behind the plant even more, but Leo wouldn't have any of this. York shouldn't be ashamed, and he shouldn't be hiding.

Leo planted himself in front of York and held out his hand. "I almost didn't see you there. Why don't we sit with the others?"

York licked his lips and looked around the table. "There's no need for me to. I don't have anything to add to this conversation."

"Maybe not, but it hasn't even started yet. Besides, no one wants you to hide in the plants. You wouldn't be here if you didn't belong."

York's cheeks flushed, but, to Leo's relief, he took his hand and allowed him to pull him to his feet. Thankfully, Tim had noticed what Leo was doing, and he'd kept two chairs next to him empty. Leo sat next to Tim, leaving the chair at the end of the table for York. That way, he'd only be sitting next to Leo, and hopefully he wouldn't feel boxed in.

As York settled in his seat and smoothed down his t-shirt, clearly trying to avoid looking up, Leo glanced around the table. Everyone was staring, and he glared at them until they stopped. Tim seemed amused, as did Marcel, but they didn't say anything about Leo's behavior.

Thank fuck for small mercies.

"Thank you, everyone, for coming," Elijah declared from his chair at the head of the table. "I know we all hoped for better news, but we haven't been able to locate Curt yet."

"How is that possible?" Jerome asked, sounding grumpy. "We know who the guy is. We know he's a cockatrice shifter. How hard can it be to find him?"

"You're welcome to try if you don't think we're doing a good enough job," Elijah said, arching a brow.

"That's not what I was saying." Jerome looked even grumpier than before, though.

"I think Jerome is saying that we're all frustrated and tired. No one has any idea where he could be?" Lindsey asked, making everyone thankful that he was there to smooth things out with Jerome.

Leo wasn't sure how Lindsey could stand being with the guy. Jerome was grumpy most of the time, and while he was fiercely protective of the people he loved and deep inside, a good person, he didn't show it often enough. He also tended to snark at people even when they didn't deserve it, and ever since York had moved in with the clan, he'd been one of his targets. Leo had been tempted to punch Jerome in the face several times. The only reason he hadn't was that Jerome was Marcel's brother.

Sometimes, Leo wondered how they could have come from the same parents.

"I'm sure he's still in town, probably plotting his next step," Elijah said, looking relieved he could talk to Lindsey rather than Jerome. "Whatever he's planning, he won't allow us to stop him. He'll try again and again until he gets what he wants, but unfortunately, that doesn't make him any easier to find."

"He could be with other cockatrice shifters," Gunter pointed out.

Everyone looked at him. He was sitting next to Elijah, looking entirely at ease.

"Are there other cockatrice shifters in town?" Donahue asked.

"There's a clan of them," Elijah confirmed. "We keep our distance. They're not exactly friendly, and we all want to avoid a war."

"We might not be able to avoid it if Curt is with them," Leo pointed out. "What do we do if that's the case?"

"Hold on," Donahue said. "Can you tell us more about this cockatrice clan? Because I can't imagine anyone would want to help Curt with whatever he's planning. Would they put their clan in danger for him?"

Leo grimaced. He'd grown up knowing the cockatrices were dangerous, but he wasn't surprised the human wasn't aware of that fact. It looked like Elijah would need to explain, if anything, to keep the humans safe.

Better him than Leo, that was for sure.

York watched as Elijah leaned back in his chair. He looked like he'd rather talk about anything but the cockatrices, which was enough to tell York he wouldn't like what he was about to hear.

"I'm sure everyone knows what cockatrices look like by now," he started. "They're kind of dragons, although they're smaller than us, and of course, they have a beak, very much like a chicken."

York doubted any cockatrice shifter would like to be called a chicken, but he kind of enjoyed thinking of Curt that way.

"So they're a lot like a dragon with a rooster's head," Elijah continued. "Some are more serpentine, others look more like dragons, but you get the idea. Dragons and cockatrice shifters have always been at each other's throats, possibly because we're the only ones who can challenge the other. Most other shifters are much smaller, so they tend to stay away from us. There's also the fact that there aren't many of either of us left. It's why we haven't fought them in years, even though we've always hated each other. No one wants to lose clan members, although I doubt it's for the same reason."

"You care about the clan, while they only care that there wouldn't be enough of them to defend their territory if they started a war," Leo said.

Elijah nodded. "Pretty much. They've always been messy, though. They have all kinds of plans but usually fail to put them into motion. I don't know about other cockatrice clans, but the one here thinks like Curt. They believe that as shifters, we should be treated better and that humans should serve us."

"Is this the clan where Curt was born?"

Elijah shrugged. "There's no way to know until we dig deeper into Curt's life. I wouldn't be surprised if they'd welcomed him even if he wasn't born here. If they share the same ideals, they can use him."

York tried to think about the time he'd spent with Curt. He'd met Melanie, Curt's girlfriend, but apart from Curt's ghostly and psychic minions, he couldn't think of anyone else. He doubted he'd ever met another cockatrice shifter, but it would be impossible to know unless they shifted in front of him. He hadn't even been sure what kind of shifter Curt was until he'd shifted in the middle of the city.

"We agree he's probably with them?" Jerome asked, looking around the table.

His gaze paused on York for a moment, and York resisted the urge to cringe away. He didn't blame Jerome for being angry after what he'd done to Marcel, but he wished Jerome didn't always look like he was about to kill him.

"I think it's a strong possibility," Elijah confirmed. "Which is what makes the situation even more complicated. Our clans are more or less balanced, which means we have the same numbers. The dragons would probably win an outright war, but it's not a given, and I can't risk it. I suspect it's why the cockatrices haven't stood behind Curt openly. They want what he's offering but can't afford to start a war with us. We have an uneasy truce, but it won't last long if we enter their territory and try to take Curt, even though we're doing it for everyone's safety. They won't see it like that."

"But they're planning on hurting the dragons," Jerome said.

"Oh, I'm sure they are. We've been enemies for decades, even though we haven't drawn each other's blood recently. They're probably supporting Curt both because of what he's doing and why he's doing it, but also because getting rid of us would mean that the entire city would become their territory. They know better than to come with us here."

"So we can't get to him, but we also can't wait for him to come to us because it would be too dangerous."

Elijah nodded. "Entering cockatrice territory is out of the question. Waiting for Curt to make his next move is dangerous, but I don't see any other alternative. Does anyone have any thoughts about this?"

The people around the table looked at each other while York stared down at the table. Maybe if he could come up with a plan, the clan would agree to it. He couldn't stop feeling as if they'd be happier to have him with them if he was more productive. Besides, he'd been the one to pull the clan into this mess. If he hadn't taken Marcel, the clan wouldn't have been involved, and York wanted to do everything in his power to make sure no one in the clan got hurt.

He cared about these people. He shouldn't, and they *definitely* shouldn't care about him, but he couldn't change how he felt. Little by little, the people around the room had started to become his friends, and if he let them in, they could become his family. He hadn't had that in a long time, and he yearned for it, but he couldn't allow the clan to be in danger.

That meant doing something about Curt.

Elijah got to his feet. "I suggest we end this meeting and think about what we know. Confirming that Curt *is* staying with the cockatrices would be good, but I won't sacrifice any of you to poke around their territory. We'll have to find another way to get that information, so if any of you has any ideas, they'd be welcome."

It made sense that Elijah didn't want to sacrifice anyone to find out more about Curt, but the easiest way to get to him would be to send someone into cockatrice territory. None of the dragons could go, but York wasn't a dragon. He also knew Curt better than anyone else in the room. He'd spent time with Curt, so he knew the guy was impulsive and thought highly of himself. Would Curt be able to tell if York lied to him?

York could get to him easily enough. He still had Curt's phone number, and while he wasn't sure Curt was still using it, it could help him anyway. At the very least, he could leave a message and see if Curt called back. If he did, York could tell him the dragons had been keeping him prisoner and that he'd managed to steal a phone from someone. He could explain he wanted out of the mansion the clan lived in and ask for his help. He'd promise to do everything Curt wanted, and Curt would probably agree. As long as York treated him like he was superior, it could work.

The people around York had started getting to their feet, but no one had left yet. They'd gathered in small groups, talking to each other and making suggestions. All of them wanted to help, but York was the one who had the best possibility of making this work. If he could get Curt away from the cockatrice clan, the dragons could swoop in and grab him. York didn't know what they'd do with him, but the world would be a better place without him.

But to obtain that, someone needed to get to Curt, and that someone would clearly need to be York, no matter what everyone thought.

He gave Leo a sideways glance. He'd be the major problem. The clan wouldn't agree to let York do this, which meant that if York truly thought it was the best he could do, he'd have to find a way out of the property and into cockatrice territory. He'd have to sneak around, and while Leo wasn't exactly stalking him, he'd be the first to notice if York tried to leave.

York didn't want to go. He didn't want to put himself in danger or to see Curt again, but it was the best thing he could do to protect the dragons and Leo.

He hadn't been able to save his brother. He wasn't sure what would happen next, but if he had to die, he hoped it would be because he was trying to save people, not because he was hurting them.

CHAPTER SIX

A few days later, York was still thinking about how to get rid of Curt. Before he could change his mind, he'd tried contacting the other man on his old number right after the meeting, but he hadn't been surprised when no one answered. He hadn't expected Curt to pick up, but he'd left a message and hoped Curt would eventually see it and reach out. He wasn't sure what he'd do when that happened, which was why he needed to start planning.

That would be easier to do if Leo wasn't in the picture. After he'd told York he cared about him and wanted to protect him, York had realized he took that very seriously. He wasn't exactly following York around, but every time York was uncomfortable, he was somehow there. They'd spent a lot of time together, making it hard for York to convince himself to do the right thing.

Leo had noticed something was up. He hadn't pushed yet, but he had to know York was planning something, and York was waiting for him to try to stop him. That was what he'd do if their roles were reversed and Leo was about to do something stupid like give himself over to their enemy.

But York had no choice. He might have to sacrifice himself if he wanted to keep the clan safe. He was ready to do it, even though Leo wouldn't be happy about it. Hell, *he* wouldn't be happy about it, either. He couldn't see another way out of this, and he was sure that eventually, Leo would understand that.

"Okay, I'm done," Leo suddenly said.

They were sitting side-by-side on York's bed, watching a movie. Or at least they were supposed to watch a movie. York hadn't been able to focus on anything but his thoughts, and he wasn't surprised that Leo had noticed.

Leo turned off the TV and turned his body to face York. He was wearing jeans and a t-shirt, and his feet were bare. He looked at ease in York's bed, as if he belonged there.

York wanted him to.

Leo stared at York. "You know you can tell me anything."

York nodded.

When he didn't say anything, Leo huffed in what had to be frustration. "Why won't you talk to me? You've been like this since the meeting. You're lost in your thoughts, and I can tell you're planning something, but I don't know what. I don't like it. I don't want you to put yourself in danger, but I suspect that's what you're planning on doing."

York's mouth was dry. "I was thinking about the situation."

"That sounds dangerous."

York glared at him, but he couldn't keep up the expression for long. "I just want you to listen to me before you start yelling, all right?"

Leo briefly closed his eyes. "Now I'm sure I'm not going to like any of this. Come on. Tell me what's going on in your head."

"Well, I know Curt. I worked with him, and I'm human. What if I called him and told him that the dragons captured me? I could say I escaped and that I need help. I'll promise to do whatever he wants, and since I'm sure he needs new psychics, he'll probably say yes and tell me where he is."

Leo got out of bed. He started pacing the space in front of it, raking a hand through his hair as he did so. "That is the worst idea I've ever heard," he said.

York cringed back against the headboard. "It's the only

way I can be useful and help the clan."

"We don't need you to be useful. We don't need you to take down Curt. The clan can do that."

York laughed, but there was no humor in it. "So you're telling me I'm useless."

"That's not what I said. You're not useless, and I think you're brave to even think about doing something like that. Can't you see it's dangerous, though? Do you really believe Curt wouldn't see right through you and know you're working with the clan?"

"He can't know for sure that I am. He didn't trust me before, and that's not going to change, but reaching out to him could give us the only opportunity we have to get to him. Besides, I don't need to go into cockatrice territory. I can tell him we'll meet somewhere."

"He won't agree to that. If he *is* in cockatrice territory, he feels safe there and won't want to give up that safety. That means you'll have to go to him, and who knows what he'll do to you? No, you can't do this."

York thought of the phone call he'd already made. Leo would be pissed if York told him about it, so York decided not to. Curt hadn't answered, anyway, so York didn't have a reason to explain all of this to Leo. "But I have to do it. It's the only way to get to Curt," he insisted.

"Why would you put yourself in danger that way?" Leo asked. He was breathing hard, as if he'd been running, and York wondered if it was fear.

He had a hard time wrapping his mind around the fact that Leo seemed to be afraid for him. Maybe he shouldn't. Leo had been clear that he was in love with him, after all.

But that was one more reason York needed to do this. He was falling in love with Leo, too, and he wanted to keep him safe. Surely Leo would understand that. "Because if I manage to do this, you and the clan will be safe. After everything you've done for me, it's the least I can do. If I do this, I can show the clan that I'm good for the clan and that I'm not trying to hurt them. Besides, maybe Jerome would finally see I didn't mean to hurt his brother."

"Who cares about what Jerome thinks?" Leo snapped. "And the clan doesn't need you to prove anything." His eyes narrowed. "Is that what you're thinking? That you need to atone and to show the clan that you're useful so we'll keep you with us?"

York looked away. Like always, Leo was right. York felt that even though the clan seemed to trust and want him, he needed to prove that he wouldn't hurt them again. He also needed to protect Leo, but that was easier said than done.

He doubted Leo would listen to him any longer. Still, he felt he had a good plan. "I can do this," he murmured.

He just hoped he was right.

Leo didn't know how to stop York from doing everything he'd just described. York had to see it would be foolish, right? He had to know that going to Curt would be too dangerous and that no one in the clan, from Leo to Elijah, wanted to risk him that way.

Leo wasn't sure about that. York was so focused on getting the clan to see he deserved everything they'd given him and on atoning for something no one blamed him for that he couldn't see what was right in front of his eyes, dammit. Leo needed to change that, but York was easily spooked. Leo wasn't sure he could avoid going all grand gesture on him, but he supposed he was about to find out how York would take it.

He stepped closer to York, who was watching him as if he expected him to yell. Leo was tempted, but York was too important to scare him away.

"You can't go," Leo said. His voice trembled, but he didn't think York noticed.

"But I could get us more information. I could help the clan take down Curt. Isn't that what everyone expects from me?"

York had already said that, but Leo refused to consider it. "No. What people expect from you is for you to settle down with the clan and find a way to be happy. No one wants you to put yourself in danger, especially when it's more probable that Curt will hurt you than for him to believe you're on his side and take advantage of you again."

York tightened his hands into fists. "But I have to do *something*."

"Not if it means putting yourself in danger, York. Please. I need you to understand that no one expects or wants you to put yourself in danger. You're too important to the clan. You're too important to *me*."

York stared at Leo for so long that Leo wondered if he'd pushed too far. York might not be ready to hear how strong Leo's feelings for him were.

Eventually, York's shoulders slumped. "Fine. It was just an idea, but I can see no one will be okay with it. I just wanted to make myself useful."

Leo narrowed his eyes. "You won't go?"

York shrugged. Leo didn't miss the fact that York hadn't told him he wouldn't reach out to Curt or even try to find him, but he doubted that pushing York in that direction would change anything. York had a stubborn streak under his soft eyes and fragile appearance, and Leo would enjoy it in any other situation.

But even though he wouldn't get a promise out of York, maybe he could *show* him that he truly didn't want him to get hurt and that he cared. He wasn't sure it was the best idea, but he didn't have any other right now, and he desperately felt the need to do something to stop York from being an idiot.

When Leo reached for York, York sucked in a breath, which caused Leo to stop moving. York didn't tell him to leave, and he didn't put more space between them, so Leo started moving again. He kept his focus on York's face to be able to see how York felt about what he was doing, but he could only read anticipation and maybe a hint of fear, which wasn't surprising.

Leo took York's hand and paused. York continued staring at him, and Leo pulled him closer, smiling when York came without resisting.

"Okay?" Leo asked as he finished pulling York into his arms.

York nodded. "Okay." His voice was barely more than a whisper, but it was enough.

Leo knew what to do, and he knew York would welcome it.

He didn't hesitate before pressing their lips together, and when York leaned into him, he delved deep with his tongue to taste the man he was falling in love with. York let out a little noise of surprise that turned Leo on even more than he already was, even though he didn't need it. York was everything he'd ever wanted in a man, down to his stubbornness and impossibility of seeing what was right in front of his eyes. Leo wouldn't have a problem making sure York knew he was loved, and not only by him.

Leo cupped the back of York's head, holding him in place as he slid his fingers into York's soft hair. It was long enough to pull, but Leo didn't dare yet. He wanted York to be more comfortable with him before deviating from the usual path.

He pressed kisses along York's jaw, using his hold on York's hair to tilt his head back so he could have easier access. He could feel York's breathing speed up and his heart racing when he kissed down his neck. It was a vulnerable position for York, but he didn't push Leo away.

He wanted this as much as Leo did.

Leo made sure to continue moving as slowly as he could. He almost expected York to stop him, but he got York's t-shirt and jeans off without him saying anything. The only thing left on York's body was his boxers, and Leo left them there—for now.

York hissed when Leo's fingertips brushed against his chest. Leo ran his hands up, avoiding York's nipples, and gently pushed him back toward the bed.

York went. He flopped onto the mattress, still staring up at Leo with wide eyes. Leo had no idea what would happen next, but he quickly shucked his jeans and t-shirt, leaving both of them in their underwear. Then he crawled onto the bed, ready to show York how much he mattered to him but unsure how to do so.

He kissed across the pale skin of York's chest, going upward again. York was perfect, but Leo knew he wouldn't believe it if he told him, so he kept his mouth shut.

There was a scar on York's collarbone. It was still pink, so it had to be recent, and when Leo reached to skim a fingertip along it, York shuddered and grabbed his wrist. He didn't push Leo's hand away but stared at him as if he didn't know what to do.

"I know it's ugly," York eventually whispered.

Leo pushed up and pressed a kiss on the scar, then on York's lips. "We all have scars. It doesn't make you any less beautiful."

York's cheeks flushed. "I don't think I'm beautiful."

"Mmm," Leo hummed. "Do you think I am? Because I don't see myself as beautiful, but I think you like what you see when you look at me."

"Of course I do. You're incredibly handsome."

Leo kissed York's scar again. "Well, I think the same of you. Neither of us sees ourselves clearly, but I see you, York. I see you, and I want you, and I believe you're the most beautiful man I've ever met. I want you, York. I want all of you, scars and past, fears and happiness. Everything."

Leo slid a hand down York's body until he found York's cock. It was hard, and while Leo wanted to look at it, it felt more important to hold York's gaze, even though it felt slightly awkward. York needed to see how much he meant to Leo.

Hopefully, it would be enough to keep him here, in Leo's arms and in his life.

Leo pushed down York's underwear until it reached mid-thigh. He didn't have the patience for more.

The feeling of York's cock in his hand sent a shiver down Leo's spine. His own cock was straining against his boxers, but he wanted to focus on York and on making him feel good. He wanted to take care of York in a way he didn't think any-one had ever done.

He didn't know what York liked yet, but he knew what he enjoyed, so he went with that, squeezing York's cock and moving his hand up and down, pausing to thumb the head of York's cock every so often.

York jerked forward, and for a moment, Leo thought he didn't want this, but York pushed his fingers under the elastic band of Leo's boxers and scrambled to free Leo's erection. Leo moaned with pleasure at the unexpectedness of it, and when his cock sprang free, he got what he wanted.

"Fuck," he muttered, trying to focus on what he was doing.

That was hard to do when York's fingers were sliding up and down his aching length.

Leo needed more. He didn't want one bit of clothes be-tween them, and unfortunately, he'd have to let go of York's cock to finish undressing both of them.

He made the sacrifice.

He let go of York's cock and pushed himself up. He quickly

finished pushing his boxers down and kicked them away before turning his attention back to York. He'd moved, too, and he was now lying on the bed completely naked. He wasn't looking at Leo, but he didn't protest when Leo took a moment to take in his body.

York truly was beautiful, with his long legs, dark happy trail, and flushed cock. Leo could still see the scar, but it didn't matter to him.

York reached for Leo. Leo understood how hard that gesture was for him, so he didn't hesitate to press down on top of York. York opened his legs and welcomed him into that groove, and it felt like Leo belonged there. No matter what York believed, he'd been made for Leo, and Leo wouldn't allow him to forget that. Every time York faltered, Leo would remind him how much he loved him.

All thought flew out of Leo's mind when York arched his back and thrust his hips up. He clung to Leo's shoulders as he bit his lower lip and undulated under him. What he wanted was clear, and Leo loved that he felt secure enough to show him this side of him.

All that mattered now was their shared pleasure. Leo loved the throaty moans coming from York, the whispered words they exchanged as they clung together and pushed each other closer to the edge of pleasure with every movement. Leo ground his hips down, grinning at the sound it got from York and at how York's cock jerked against his.

York pushed up to kiss Leo. Leo's rhythm faltered, but only for a second, and it didn't matter anyway. Warmth burst in the space between their stomach, making every movement slick. When the head of Leo's cock slid against York's, he could feel how slick it was. It was still twitching, and Leo grinned against York's lips.

He'd done that. He'd made York cry out in pleasure. He'd brought him to this point and had made him feel good.

He buried his hand into York's hair and held him in place as he plunged his tongue between York's lips. York moaned, and his legs tightened around Leo's hips. When he pushed their groins harder together, Leo tilted over the edge, groaning as he came.

It took Leo a moment to recover, but even when he did, he didn't go anywhere. He rolled them to their sides and used the sheet to clean them up. A shower would be better, but they could take one later or tomorrow morning. He was afraid to let go of York, almost as if all of this would disappear if he did.

He settled them into a comfortable position, him on his back with York snuggled against his side. His arm was around York's shoulders, holding him close. Leo kissed the top of York's hair and took a deep breath. The room smelled of them and of sex, and it was perfect.

"You are loved," he murmured. "You're important to the clan and to me. I don't care how many times I have to tell you that. I'll repeat it until you believe me."

York didn't answer. Maybe he was already asleep, or maybe he didn't know what to say. Either way, Leo would keep the promise he'd just made.

CHAPTER SEVEN

York hadn't changed his mind. How could he, when he owed everything to the clan? The only way to thank them for everything they'd done for him was to help them get rid of Curt, whatever that meant. York couldn't kill him himself—he didn't have the guts to do that—but there was something he *could* do.

At the very least, he could try to find out what Curt's plan was. He'd told York and the other psychics before, and whatever he was doing now, he'd need help. York wasn't sure Curt would believe him when he told him that the dragons had kept him prisoner, but he'd decided to send Curt's old number another message anyway. It had taken him a while to come up with it because he'd kept deleting words and typing them again. He wanted Curt to think he was getting desperate and that the dragons wouldn't hesitate to hurt him. Hell, he'd insinuated they already had.

All of this was harder after what had happened between him and Leo. Even though York knew this was the right thing to do, he found that he didn't want to do it anymore. It would take him away from Leo, and that would make the dragon angry. He might not want anything to do with York when York managed to come back.

If he managed to come back.

York had no doubt that if Curt found out what he was trying to do, he'd kill him. That wouldn't be enough to stop York.

He'd made sure not to tell anyone anything. No one knew, not Elijah, not Tim, and certainly not Leo. York didn't know

75

what was growing between the two of them, but he liked to think of Leo as his boyfriend, even though they hadn't talked about it. He wasn't sure they'd ever get to that point, considering what he was about to do.

His phone had vibrated moments earlier, startling him. He was lucky he'd been alone, because the text he'd received meant his plan was a go. Curt had sent him a phone number, which York was expected to call. He'd been fighting with himself, but he couldn't wait any longer if he didn't want Curt to get suspicious.

It would be a damn miracle if he wasn't already.

His fingers shook as he clicked on the number in the text, and when his phone asked if he wanted to call, he agreed, then raised the phone to his ear. He wasn't sure he was ready to hear Curt's voice again. He had nightmares about it, but there was no way out of this.

"I didn't think you'd call," Curt said as he answered.

York swallowed. "I wasn't sure I'd be able to. I had to steal this phone, and I don't know how they haven't noticed yet."

"So the dragons have you?"

"Yeah. They took me to this home, and they're keeping me locked up in a bedroom. They're feeding me, but they had a lot of questions about you, and they weren't happy I didn't have any information." That was mostly the truth, except for the bit about him being locked up. The only reason he'd barely left his bedroom was that he hadn't wanted to, but he'd known he'd be welcome to.

"I'm not saving your ass."

York almost snorted. He hadn't expected anything different. "I'm not asking you to. I'm pretty sure I can sneak out on my own. I've befriended one of the dragons, which is how I got his phone. I told him I was calling my brother."

"Your brother's dead."

The words were like a punch to the stomach. "But they

don't know that. I said I wanted to reassure my brother that I was all right, and they let me do it. I think I can get out of here. I just don't know where to go once I do."

"That's why you contacted me? Because you need a place to stay?"

"Yes. I don't think I can go far. I don't have any money or a car. I don't have a home since I've been with you for a while."

"I'm not a hotel."

"I promise I won't stay long. I just need a few days to stay out of sight and get my feet under me. Then, I'll be out of your hair." York hesitated, hoping Curt was falling for this. "Unless you need my help again? You're still planning all that stuff, aren't you?"

"I'm not planning anything," Curt snapped. "But I might have a use for you. That is, if you manage to come without the dragons attached to your ass."

"I'll do everything I can."

"Fine. I'll help you, but first, I want to see you. I don't know if I can trust you."

York wasn't sure if he was relieved or horrified that Curt seemed to be falling for this. "I'm a prisoner. If I leave, I can't come back. You need to give me a safe place to lay low for a few days."

"I don't care what you need. You'll do as I say when I say it, or you'll be on your own on the streets. Got it?"

He hadn't changed, had he? York had wondered if getting his ass kicked in front of half the city would have made him change his ways, but he should have known better. Curt was an asshole, and he'd always be one. He took advantage of people, used them to do things he didn't want to do himself, and once he was done, he discarded them and threw them away.

"As long as you're not lying to me, you'll be safe for a bit,"

Curt said. "But you better obey my orders."

"Didn't I before? I know what you expect from me, Curt. Between you and the dragons, I'd rather be with you."

"Damn right. They're monsters."

York almost told him to fuck off. He might have if he hadn't kept in mind that he was doing this for the clan.

The dragons were the opposite of Curt, and it was a good thing. York could only imagine what would have happened to him if they hadn't taken him in. He might be about to find out. They'd have no way to know where he went, and while he hoped to be able to come back once his meeting with Curt was over, he wasn't an idiot. Curt was dangerous, and there was a chance he'd kill him rather than tell him what was going on.

Whatever happened next, York was about to find out.

He and Curt hung up after Curt said he'd send York another text with an address where they'd meet. As soon as he had it, York looked it up so he'd know where he was going. He had an idea about where cockatrice territory was, and he was pretty sure he wasn't wrong when he realized that this place was either right smack in the middle of it or on its border.

It would be dangerous. If Curt even had an inkling that York was betraying him, he wouldn't hesitate to kill him, and no one would know where York had gone. It was almost enough to keep him in his room, but instead, he grabbed his jacket, put on his shoes, and snuck out.

He'd been watching the clan, so he knew most people were busy at this time of day. When he walked downstairs, he could hear the sound of people working in the kitchen, getting dinner ready. Leo was outside, busy at the back of the house, so York wouldn't see him before leaving. He was sorry about that, but he couldn't afford for Leo to realize what he was doing. He would if he took one look at York.

It was better not to risk it, and York realized how lucky he was that no one saw him on his way out. He managed to sneak out of the house without anyone stopping him. From there, it was easy to get to the gate and pass it.

Once he was on the street, he looked around. It had been a while since he'd been away from the clan, but he knew where he was. He'd made sure he did.

He sucked in a breath. If he wanted to get to Curt quickly, he had to move, even though he felt he was leaving his heart behind.

He was pretty sure he was.

Most of Leo's body ached by the time he was done working, but it felt good to have a day's job under his belt and be able to relax. He made his way toward the house, smiling when he opened the back door and the smell of food hit him, making his stomach grumble. He was starving, but he needed a shower before he was ready to eat. He'd also pick up York from his bedroom, and maybe today, York would agree to come downstairs and eat with everyone else.

Leo didn't want to push him, but he felt that it was what York needed. No matter how many times everyone told him he was part of the clan, he wouldn't believe it until he saw it, and that wouldn't happen if he kept on hiding. Leo had been working on convincing him to take time away from his bedroom, and he hoped he'd succeed today. He wanted to see his family, maybe to introduce York to his parents. They'd been asking him about York because they'd noticed he was spending a lot of time with him, but he hadn't wanted to tell them anything. He wasn't sure where he and York stood and wouldn't be until they talked, but he didn't know if that would happen tonight. He just wanted to spend the evening with York. Surely, that wasn't too much to ask.

He quickly went through his routine of going back to his bedroom, showering with water as hot as he could stand it, then putting on a clean pair of jeans and a sweater. Since he was leaving his room, he put on socks and a pair of shoes he never used outside the house, then went to York's bedroom.

When he knocked, no one answered. That was strange because even when he felt like being alone, York always opened his door or, at the very least, asked who it was. Maybe someone else had come by and convinced him to go downstairs. Tim was the only one who could manage that, and he had a few times, so Leo wasn't overly worried as he headed back downstairs, straight to the dining hall.

It was already full of people, although most of them hadn't started eating yet. They were gathered in small groups, chatting and catching up after being away from each other for the entire day. Most of the clan dragons worked outside the house, in the city, and while they were adults, it felt good to have everyone back under the same roof. Leo wasn't close to all of them by any means, but they were still part of his clan, and it meant something.

He spied Marcel sitting on a window seat on his own, so he went that way. His best friend looked up when he heard him and smiled, and Leo flopped next to him, leaning against the cold stone of the wall. He briefly closed his eyes and sighed in relief, happy to be off his feet.

"You look tired," Marcel commented.

"That's because I am."

"You just came in?"

"Yeah. I checked on the greenhouse before going to shower, and everything is growing as it should."

Marcel had taken an interest in growing his own vegetables, but he hadn't known where to start, so Leo had pitched in to help him. He was serious enough about it, but nothing like Leo. Leo hadn't expected him to be. He was pretty sure

Marcel had decided to do it to distract himself from the night-mares and the memories of what had happened when he'd been in Curt's hands, but it didn't always help.

"Where's your better half?" Marcel asked, the teasing obvious in his voice and expression.

Leo found himself smiling. "Please tell me you're talking about York."

Marcel laughed. "Who else? Unless you've been hiding something from me?"

"I promise I'm not. To answer your question, I don't know where York is. He didn't open when I knocked on his door, so I thought he'd be here with Tim."

Marcel frowned. "I haven't seen either of them."

"I'm sure Tim is getting York in trouble. It's nothing to worry about." But Leo's stomach churned. York hadn't texted him to tell him what was going on, but he usually did. Was today different for some reason? Maybe Tim hadn't given York the time to warn Leo. Besides, it wasn't like he had to. He was an adult, and he could decide what he wanted to do with his day and that he didn't want to call Leo and tell him about it.

"Even though you said it was nothing to worry about, you look worried," Marcel pointed out.

Leo shook himself and plastered a smile on his face. "I guess I'm just a bit anxious. York has been talking about doing something to show the clan he means well, and while he agreed not to do anything stupid, I wouldn't put it past him."

Marcel's expression turned serious. "What was he planning exactly?"

"He wanted to give himself up to Curt and act as if we'd held him prisoner. He hoped that would be enough for Curt to take him back in and tell him about his plans."

"I doubt Curt would tell anyone about his plans, least of all York. No offense, but it was obvious York wasn't exactly on board with what Curt was doing."

"I know. I convinced York not to do it." But now, he was having doubts. He got to his feet. "I'm going upstairs to knock on his door again and try to convince him to come to eat with us. If you see him, can you tell him I'm looking for him?"

"Of course. And if I see Tim, I'll ask him if he knows where York is."

"Thanks."

Leo didn't have the patience to stay in the dining room for a moment longer. He didn't feel right, and he didn't know what it meant, or rather, he didn't want to think about what it meant. Surely York hadn't been so stupid as to go to Curt.

Right?

Leo climbed the stairs two-by-two, in a hurry to get to York. York's bedroom door was still closed when Leo reached it, and he quickly knocked, hoping and praying York would answer. When no one did, he decided that maybe York was asleep.

He knocked again, then tried the handle. York didn't usually lock the door, but Leo was cautious as he pushed it open and peeked inside.

York was nowhere to be seen. The bedroom was empty, as was the bathroom. Leo could see it because the door was open, but he still stepped in and checked. He even checked the shower, but York wasn't there.

Where was he, then?

Leo took his phone out before he got back into the hallway. He dialed Tim's number as he tried thinking about where York could have gone. Maybe they'd missed each other, and he was looking for Leo?

"What's up?" Tim answered.

Leo turned toward his bedroom. "Have you seen York?"

"Isn't he in his room?"

"He's not. I can't find him."

"Have you looked outside? He likes to sit on that stone bench and try to find his brother."

Leo should have thought of that spot way sooner. "I'm going there right now."

"I'll look around the house and ask everyone I see." There was urgency in Tim's voice, and it echoed in Leo's chest.

Where was York? Why hadn't he told anyone where he was going?

Leo and Tim hung up, and Leo tried calling York. He knew something was wrong when there was no answer. York always answered, even if Leo only texted him a funny cat picture. It was as if he was afraid Leo would think he didn't care if he didn't, and Leo had made sure to reassure him he didn't have to rush his answer the way he had.

He hoped York wasn't answering because he'd taken his words to heart, but what would be the odds?

York had been relieved to discover the address Curt had given him wasn't in cockatrice territory. The coffee shop was just outside of it, and while that was reassuring, its position also made York nervous. It wouldn't take much for Curt to drag him into cockatrice territory, and what would he do then?

Maybe coming here hadn't been such a good idea. His phone had started vibrating in his pocket a while ago now, and he'd peeked at it a few times, not at all surprised to see Leo's name flashing on the screen. Tim's had, too, and York thought it was a sure sign they'd realized he wasn't anywhere in the house. They were looking for him, but he couldn't afford to answer and explain what was happening. They'd rush to him right away, not giving him the chance to find out what Curt was up to.

York needed to.

He'd been nursing a cup of coffee for almost half an hour when the coffee shop door opened. He'd looked up every time he heard it, but until now, it had been other customers.

Curt walked in.

York's mouth instantly went dry, and he took a sip of his cold coffee in an attempt to make it stop. Curt looked around for a moment before finding him, and when he did, he made his way toward him. York knew Curt wouldn't hurt him in a public place, but he still couldn't bring himself to look up at the guy until he stopped by his table.

"You're here," Curt said.

York licked his lips. "I said I would be."

"I wasn't sure you'd be able to get out of the house." Curt dragged the chair on the other side of the table away and slid into it. "The dragons don't seem like the kind to let you go just because you ask nicely."

"I didn't ask. I snuck out, just like I said I would."

"Right, because one of the dragons has a crush on you."

York thought of Leo. "I don't know if it's a crush or something else, and I don't care." He very much did, but he needed to steel himself and control his emotions. If he wanted this to work—and he did—he had to focus on getting information out of Curt.

"What do you expect from me?" Curt asked.

"Just what I said on the phone. It would be great if you could give me a safe place to stay for a few days until I find a way out of the city."

Curt tapped his fingertips onto the table as he stared at York. "You mentioned something about wanting to work with me."

The thought of working with him again made York want to throw up, possibly in Curt's lap. The guy deserved it. "I need money. I want to get away from this place, but I'm not going anywhere unless I have money to pay for food, a mode of transportation, and an apartment or a motel room. Do you have something for me?"

Curt stared for a moment before nodding. "I think I do. Follow me."

He got up, and York scrambled to go after him. Curt didn't look back once or wait for York. He obviously knew that if York wanted this, he'd be right behind him.

There was nothing York wanted less, but he didn't say it out loud. He couldn't afford to. Instead, he followed Curt out of the coffee shop and toward the alley behind it. He was nervous about being alone with Curt, but he needed to deal with it and focus on his plan. If he could get Curt to explain what he needed him for before they reached whatever place they were headed to, he could go home and tell the clan about it. That was all he wanted and the only reason he was here.

They turned into the alley, and Curt gestured. "Climb in."

York stared at the white van parked there. He doubted he'd ever see Leo again if he got in. "Where are we going?" Maybe he could use up enough time that Curt would feel he wasn't worth it.

"I'll tell you when we're there."

"This doesn't feel like a good idea. I just need money."

Curt stepped closer, looming over York. "You said you'd help me."

"Yeah, but it doesn't feel like a good idea anymore. You know what? Let's forget about all of this. You'll go back to whatever you were doing, and I'll find my way out of town."

York's heart raced as he looked around, trying to find an escape route. The van blocked most of the alley, but he was pretty sure he could go around it. He was small, while Curt was bulkier, so maybe Curt would get stuck and give York enough time to run. The only other option would be to go back where they came from, but Curt was standing in the middle of the alley, blocking that route.

York inched toward the van, never looking away from Curt. "Look, I'm grateful you agreed to see me, but it's better if I go."

"But you said you'd help me."

The back doors of the van popped open. York started turning to see what was happening, but he already knew. He should have expected Curt not to come alone. He'd thought that since Curt wasn't afraid of him, he'd be able to talk his way out of this, but he'd been an idiot.

And now he was going to pay.

Two burly men dropped out of the van. If York had to guess, he'd say they were cockatrice shifters. It would make sense, since the clan suspected Curt was hiding with them.

York swallowed. "I'm useless. You always told me that."

"Maybe, maybe not. I'm sure that if I can't find a good use for you, my friends will."

Curt nodded at the men, and they each grabbed one of York's arms. York tried running, but he couldn't pull away from them, and when they dragged him toward the van, he knew he'd lost.

They pushed him inside. He stumbled and fell, barely managing to catch himself on his hands. He turned and tried to scramble out, but Curt stood in front of him, his arms crossed over his chest.

"Did you think I'd believe you?"

York hoped he looked as innocent as he was trying to appear. "I don't know what you're talking about."

"I know the dragons. Those assholes like to think they're better than us. They'd never have locked you up, and if they had, they'd have let you go a while ago. What reason would they have to keep you around?" He leaned so close that York could smell the coffee on his breath. "You thought I was an idiot, but you're the one in trouble now."

It was useless to continue acting as if York didn't know

what was happening. "They'll come for me."

Curt laughed. "Why should they? You hurt one of theirs, and they don't take kindly to that. I don't know why they kept you, but you're clearly not useful to them anymore since they sent you back. I'm sure they thought it was good riddance."

But the clan hadn't sent York back to Curt. York had done that entirely on his own, and he could see how stupid he'd been. The problem was that he didn't think he could escape.

One of the burly guys hopped out of the back of the van, and he and Curt slammed the door shut. York moved toward them before they could, but the guy who'd stayed with him in the van grabbed his arm and pulled him back. York tried to fight, and the guy's hand tightened painfully, no doubt leaving a bruise.

"Stop fighting," the guy said. His voice was softer than York had expected and almost gentle. "It's not going to help you right now."

York could tell he was right. He slumped down, and the guy let him go. York didn't have the time to try for the doors again because Curt and the other guy climbed in the front, Curt in the passenger seat. The other guy took the wheel, and York could only stare outside the windshield and try to convince himself that Curt had been lying.

The clan *would* come for him. They had to.

But how would they find him if they didn't know where he'd gone?

York wasn't anywhere on the clan's property. Leo was sure of it because he'd gone everywhere, from York's bedroom to the bench in the yard he liked to sit on. He hadn't been able to find him, and neither had Tim, who'd kept him updated through text messages.

They met again in the dining hall. It was getting late, and

almost everyone was done eating. It meant the room was mostly empty and that Leo could break down without too many people seeing him.

"Nothing?" Tim asked.

Leo shook his head and flopped onto one of the chairs at the table where Jerome, Will, Lindsey, Victor, and Marcel were already sitting. "He's not here. He left." That was the only explanation Leo could think of.

Tim stopped next to Leo. "Why would he have left? I know he wasn't entirely happy here, but surely, it was better than what he'd have out there."

Leo rubbed his face. "I know why he left. He wasn't running from the clan. He went back to Curt."

Tim looked horrified. "Why would he do that?"

"Because he wants to be useful and to show the clan that he can truly be one of us."

"But he already is."

"I know that as well as you, but he's never been convinced. I don't know what to do, Tim. I want to go after him, but if we're right and Curt is with the cockatrices, we can't just burst in."

Tim was already nodding. "I called Elijah. He should be here soon, and hopefully he can help us find a way out of this."

Leo didn't care about anything but getting York back. If he had to, he'd sneak into cockatrice territory alone. From Tim's expression, though, he doubted he would have to. Tim would be here for him, but even more so, he'd be there for York. That was who mattered to Tim, and Leo was glad for that.

The sound of footsteps made both of them look up. Elijah appeared at the door, wearing sleeping pants and a t-shirt. Leo couldn't remember the last time he'd seen Elijah dressed like that, but then Elijah was their leader. He tended to dress conservatively and keep his behavior serious. He wasn't always that way, and it felt good to see him differently tonight. He seemed more approachable, and that was what Leo needed with York gone.

"What's going on?" Elijah asked, sitting at the table with them.

"York is gone," Leo told him. "We can't find him anywhere, and he was talking about reaching out to Curt so he could find out more about his plans. He wanted to make himself useful to the clan."

"Are we sure about that?" Jerome snarked. "Maybe he learned everything he could from us and went back to Curt to tell him all about the clan."

Leo was pretty sure he'd have punched Jerome in the face if Marcel hadn't put a hand on his arm. Once Leo settled, Marcel turned to glare at his brother. "How can you say something like that?"

Jerome looked bashful, but unfortunately, it only lasted a few seconds. "Think about it. We all fell for it, but isn't it weird that he changed his mind about hurting you? Why would he have agreed to come here if it wasn't to gather information?"

"He feels guilty," Leo snapped. "You haven't talked to him recently, have you? He knows the clan has given him an opportunity he wouldn't have had without us. He wants to be useful and to help the clan, to atone for what he did to Marcel, no matter how many times Marcel tells him he doesn't need to. *That's* why he left—because he wanted to show Elijah and assholes like you that he could be useful to the clan. I hope you're happy."

"I had nothing to do with this. I don't know where your boyfriend went, but as far as I'm concerned, it's good riddance."

Leo slammed both palms on top of the table and started climbing onto it, needing to get to Jerome and strangle him with his bare hands. Marcel grabbed Leo from behind while Tim pushed him back from his seat next to Jerome.

"Enough," Elijah snapped, getting everyone's attention.

Leo tried lunging at Jerome again, but one glare from Elijah sent him back in his chair.

"I know you don't trust York," Elijah told Jerome. "But you're the only one who feels that way. Even your brother forgave him for what he did, so why don't you try to see things without the layer of anger and resentment you have for him?" Elijah turned to Leo. "As for you, I don't take kindly to physical fights in my home."

Leo hung his head. "I apologize, Alpha."

"And please, don't call me that. I know you didn't mean to hurt Jerome."

Leo had, but he was pretty sure that admitting it wouldn't help, so he nodded and kept his mouth shut.

Elijah pinched the bridge of his nose for a moment before nodding. "All right. Tell me where you looked and why you think he left."

Leo explained the plan York had come up with a few days ago after the meeting. He told everyone around the table that he'd looked for York everywhere, including in the yard, but he wasn't there. Tim added a few things, but there was nothing much to say. York was gone.

Leo was going to spank him once he got him back.

He swallowed. "We're dating," he added. "I know some of you don't care about him, but I do, and I'll go alone if I have to. I hope I'll have the clan's support for this, though. We've been telling York time and time again that he's one of us and that we want him here, but it's clear some people don't, and I don't want him to have to see that. If the clan wants to wash its hands of York, I'll leave with him once I get him back."

Elijah was already shaking his head. "I told York he was a clan member, and I meant it. I don't care that some people don't trust him. I talked to him several times, and he knows that what he did was wrong. I'm sure Jerome would understand and feel more compassion for what York has gone through if he tried putting himself in his shoes and imagining Marcel in Cooper's place."

Leo glanced at Jerome to see the man's reaction. To his surprise, Jerome looked uncomfortable rather than angry. Leo had no idea what that meant, and right now, he didn't care.

"What will we do?" Leo asked, looking around their table.

Elijah sighed. "If Curt has him, he'll have no doubt taken him back to the cockatrices. I'll try reaching out to them and ask about York. He's a clan member, and they have no right to take him. I doubt it'll change anything, though. We might have to go to war with them if we want York back."

Leo gritted his teeth. "And you're unwilling to do that."

Elijah's expression was fierce. "We don't leave anyone behind. What kind of clan leader would I be if I hesitated to fight to get York back? I'd hoped it wouldn't come to war, but it won't be our fault even if it does. I don't care what it takes. York *will* come home."

Leo breathed easier, but he was still worried. It was too easy to imagine what the cockatrices were doing to York and what would happen if things truly came down to a war. He agreed with Elijah, though. He wouldn't hesitate to attack cockatrice territory if it meant getting York back.

And fuck anyone who tried to stop him.

CHAPTER EIGHT

Y ork stared out the window. The sun was peeking above
the trees, and he thought about what was happening
back home. People were no doubt waking up right now, getting ready to go to work. What was Leo doing?

He'd have noticed York was gone. They spent their eve-
nings together, watching TV or cuddling in bed and talking.
He was probably panicking, and York wished he'd thought
better of this. He didn't want Leo to feel that way.

He also didn't want to be locked up in this bedroom, but
they'd taken his phone, so he was stuck.

He looked around, but nothing had changed since the last
time he had. He was still in a mostly empty bedroom with
only a bed by the window and a small table. There was also a
chair, but one of the legs was cracked, and York didn't dare
sit on it.

He supposed he was lucky there was a bathroom. That
way, he hadn't had to pee out the window. York would have
done it, too, and he wouldn't have cared if one of the guards
had been walking under the window when he had. The punishment would have hurt, but he'd have gotten so much sat-
isfaction out of that.

But there *was* a bathroom, and he'd made good use of it.
What he hadn't done was eat the food the guy who'd ridden
in the van next to him had brought a few hours after they'd
arrived.

York didn't know where he was. He was sure they were in
cockatrice territory, but he hadn't been able to see much when

he'd been in the van, and as soon as he'd climbed out of it, he'd been pushed toward this house. It was surrounded by trees, and as far as York could see, no one else was around.

He'd been looking out the window most of the night, so he knew Curt and one of the guys who'd taken him had left. The only one who hadn't was the guy who'd been in the back of the van with York, and he'd been nice enough, something that puzzled York.

What was the guy doing? Why was he being so nice when it was clear Curt hated York?

York gently tapped his forehead against the cool glass of the window. He should have known better. No matter how arrogant Curt was, he wasn't an idiot. He'd seen right through York and had turned the tables on him. Now, Curt was the one in charge.

Had York ever been?

He'd thought he had when he'd told Curt that bullshit about the dragons taking him, but he suspected Curt had seen right through him from the first text he'd sent.

The sound of the door opening made York jump up from the bed. He pressed his back against the wall next to the window and watched as the guy from the night before walked in, carrying a tray. He came closer to put it down on the table, frowning when he saw York hadn't eaten anything last night.

"You must be hungry," he murmured.

"I'm not eating anything you give me. I don't know what you've put in it."

The guy shook his head. "I swear I haven't put anything in your food, and I'm the only one here. Curt left last night, and he hasn't been back yet."

"But he will eventually."

The guy nodded. "And soon. I'm sure you want to keep up your strength so you can deal with him."

York stared at the man. He didn't understand him, but

maybe he didn't have to. "I'm York."

The guy hesitated. "Terrence," he eventually said.

"I'd say it was a pleasure meeting you, but it's not."

Terrence chuckled. "I don't blame you. I wish I weren't in this situation, too, but there's no way out for us. You should eat. I promise there's nothing in the food."

"You could let me go," York quickly said when Terrence turned toward the door after grabbing last night's tray.

Terrence paused. "I'm sorry. I can't."

"You could just look the other way. I'd sneak out, and you could tell Curt that."

"I can't risk my family."

All the fight bled out of York. Of course Terrence had a family, and of course they were more important to him than York could ever be. York didn't blame him. He'd have betrayed anyone if it meant saving his brother.

Terrence left, and while York believed that he hadn't put anything in the food, he wasn't hungry. He ate a few bites of eggs and half a slice of bread, but that was all. He might have eaten more if he hadn't heard the sound of a car stopping in front of the house. When he peered out, it was to see Curt had arrived.

York swallowed.

He was about to find out what Curt would do with him.

He got to his feet, not wanting to be sitting down and give Curt the advantage. He held his breath as he listened to Curt walk into the house, then upstairs. He raised his chin high when the door opened and Curt appeared.

Curt didn't even look at the tray. He probably didn't care if York ate or let himself starve.

"Terrence told me you didn't try to escape during the night," Curt said.

"I'm sure you have guards ready to intervene if I as much think of running away."

Curt laughed. "I don't have guards. The cockatrices do, though, and they're not going to give you up easily. You're a nice hostage."

York swallowed. "Why? You said the dragons wouldn't come for me."

"And I still believe they won't, but I'm not the one in charge, unfortunately. You're not going anywhere for the time being." His smile widened. "But I haven't been forbidden from using you. Now, what should I do with you?"

York's chest felt tight, but he forced himself to appear relaxed. "Nothing. You always said I was useless. Besides, I don't want to work for you. It was all a lie."

"I'm aware of that. You're a shitty liar. But you could come in handy. You see, I don't have as many psychics working for me as before. Those dragons almost ruined everything, which means I need help. It's good that you suddenly dropped in my lap, isn't it?"

York shook his head. "Didn't you hear me? I'm not helping you."

Curt moved so quickly that York barely had the time to steel himself. He grabbed York's throat and slammed him against the wall so hard that York briefly wondered if the wall could stand it. Was there going to be a York-sized hole in it by the time Curt was done with him?

"Now you listen to me, and listen good," Curt murmured as he leaned closer to York's ear. "You'll do what I tell you when I tell you to do it."

"No." York would have said yes only a few months ago, but now, he had something to fight for. He'd hurt Marcel, and he wouldn't allow Curt to push him into hurting someone else.

Curt threw York on the floor. York had the time to see him raise his leg, so he knew the kick was coming. He curled himself into a tight ball, expecting the pain. When it came, it knocked the air out of his lungs. He shuddered, then tried to protect his head with his arms.

Thankfully for him, Curt didn't spend much time beating him. Apparently, scaring York half to death was enough for him to feel satisfied, and maybe he truly had plans for York and didn't want to hurt him too badly.

"You'll change your mind," Curt promised. "And if you don't, well, you won't be useful to me anymore, and you know what I do with people who aren't useful to me."

York did. He'd seen it several times, and the dark promise was enough to freak him out.

He stayed where he was as he listened to Curt leave the room. The door slammed shut behind him, and the sound of the lock told him he could finally relax.

But could he? He'd sworn to himself he'd never hurt the clan or anyone else again, and he wanted to keep that promise, but he also didn't want to die.

It looked like he was going to have to choose between those two options.

It was early in the morning, but Leo was already exhausted. He hadn't slept last night, instead pacing the length of his bedroom while thinking about York. He wanted to go out there and find him right away, but Elijah had forbidden him and everyone else to do something that stupid, and in the light of day, he understood why. He didn't like it, but putting himself in danger and needing the clan to rescue one more person wouldn't help anyone, least of all York.

So Leo had paced and thought about York and what he was going through. Hopefully, Curt had left him alone for the night, and York was safe. Even if that was true, it would change soon. It was morning, and everyone was waking up, including monsters like Curt.

As soon as it wasn't too early, Leo left his bedroom. He headed straight for the dining hall, needing coffee to start his day. They had a meeting in about an hour, and while he wanted nothing more than to bypass that, the coffee, and everything else and run to York's rescue, Leo wouldn't be able to do all of that on his own. He needed help. He needed the clan, and the only way to get them on board was to talk to them, or rather, to Elijah.

They wouldn't be telling the entire clan what had happened. Only the people dealing with Curt and his cronies needed to be informed. They were the ones who would no doubt try to rescue York, and Leo felt better knowing he wasn't alone. He wasn't a hundred percent sure about Jerome, but if Marcel asked, Jerome would be the first in line to rescue York. He'd bitch about it, but it wouldn't make his help any less valuable.

Leo drank his first cup of coffee, then got a refill and sat next to the window, staring outside. He wouldn't go to work today, but no one would expect him to. He didn't care about the garden if he couldn't have York in it. He'd already known he was in love with York, but having him disappear like this had made it impossible for him to ignore. He wasn't sure what it meant or what he'd do about it once all of this was over and York was home, but he supposed the only option was to love York and make sure he knew about his feelings.

Leo wasn't angry that York had gone on his own. He understood why York felt the way he did, why he needed to prove himself no matter how many times Leo and the others told him it wasn't necessary. Leo couldn't say he wouldn't have felt the same way if he'd been in York's place. Going on his own had been stupid, though, as had thinking he could somehow fool Curt into thinking he was on his side. Even someone who didn't know York as well as Leo did would know there was no way York would be on board with hurting people.

"Did you sleep?" Tim asked as he sat in the chair next to Leo's.

"I don't think I could have closed my eyes even if I'd tried."

Tim grimaced. He was holding his own cup of coffee and took a few sips before turning his attention back to Leo. "You're not going to be of much use if we have to attack the cockatrices. You should have slept."

Leo glared at him. "What if Victor had been taken? Would you have been able to sleep?"

"Hell, no. I don't think Elijah will want to go today, anyway, so you have time to rest."

Leo frowned. "What do you mean, he won't want to go today?"

"Exactly that. We have to gather information on Curt and the cockatrices, on their territory, and find a way inside. There's no way Elijah will want to do this without taking time to go through everything that could go wrong and every way we can make it right. He might have accepted that we can't avoid a war with the cockatrices, but he won't be stupid about it."

Leo wanted to scream that they couldn't leave York with Curt for that long, but he pressed his lips together instead. York had acted impulsively without consulting anyone, and now, he was in trouble. It wouldn't help for Leo to do something just as stupid and go out there to confront the cockatrices without his clan by his side.

Elijah was the clan leader. He was the one who made decisions, and Leo needed to follow them, no matter how much he didn't like them. Elijah would probably turn a blind eye if Leo did something he wasn't supposed to, but he'd never forgive Leo if he put the clan in danger, even if it was for the sake of the man he loved.

Elijah was understanding and wanted everyone to be safe

and happy, but the clan came first, always.

"Let's head to the meeting," Tim said as he got to his feet.

They both got another coffee before heading out. Leo wanted to run, to do something that would help York, and he felt awful just walking down the hallway heading to a meeting. On his own, though, he couldn't do anything. It would be too risky, and it wouldn't help York if he put himself in danger and got himself killed. York needed Leo, which meant Leo had to be smart.

The thought that York might get hurt while Leo waited made him want to throw up, but he reminded himself that this was the only way to do this. Curt probably didn't think the dragons would enter cockatrice territory, and they had to use that to their advantage. Besides, York was strong. He'd survived Curt once, and Leo was sure he could do it a second time. After that, he'd make sure York never left his bedroom again.

Or at least, that was what he wished he could do. The best way to lose York would be to clip his wings, though, and Leo was going to have to learn to live with everything that was happening and the consequences.

Luckily, it seemed that everyone knew how urgent the situation was. When he and Tim reached the conference room, most people involved in the fight with the cockatrices and Curt were already there. One of Victor's brothers was missing, along with Gunter, but both arrived quickly. Elijah had been sitting at the head of the table, and he frowned at Gunter as he sat next to him. He didn't say anything, and Leo didn't ask what was happening. He had other people to focus on.

"Leo, why don't you tell us what York did?" Elijah said, opening the meeting.

Not everyone in the room knew what had happened to York, so Leo quickly went through it again. He explained about York's plan and how he'd acted as if he wouldn't do anything, then had promptly turned around and left on his own. Once Leo was done, Elijah took over, explaining about the conversation they'd had last night and what they believed had happened to York. Once he was done, the room stayed silent for a bit, everyone staring at each other.

"So you believe York is in cockatrice territory," Gunter said slowly.

"It's the only thing that makes sense. We weren't sure Curt went there, but I don't see another explanation."

"I agree. What will you do about it?"

"We need to get York back," Leo said, as if the people in the room had forgotten that was why they were there.

Gunter nodded. "I agree. I'm just not sure how we're going to do it. Just yesterday, Elijah told us that he didn't want to start a war with the cockatrices. Isn't that what will happen if we do anything about this?"

Elijah sighed. "It is, but I don't see any other option. York is in danger, and I won't abandon a clan member just because he did something stupid."

Jerome snorted, but thankfully, he didn't say anything about just how stupid York had been. Maybe it was because Marcel glared at him, or maybe because Elijah looked at him like he wanted to slap him upside the head.

Leo was tempted to do just that.

"We're going to have to sneak in," Marcel said. "That way, we won't start an open war with the cockatrices. They won't believe us if we tell them we have nothing to do with York vanishing from their territory, but they won't have proof. If they attack us, they'll be in the wrong, and we need that to be the case when the time comes to deal with the human authorities."

Leo wasn't sure how useful it would be, but he supposed it would be better than nothing.

Elijah slowly nodded. "I agree. We need to keep things as

much on our side as we can. If they're the aggressors, we'll be in the right if something happens."

Leo understood everything everyone was saying, but he still wanted to scream. "What do we do, then?" he asked.

"We start planning," Elijah said. There was a promise in his words, and Leo believed that he'd do everything he could to get York back.

He had to.

There wasn't much for York to do. He'd spent most of the morning staring at the wall, then he'd moved on to staring at the door. Terrence had come around with lunch, but York wasn't hungry. He appreciated what Terrence was doing as much as he hated the guy. He wanted Terrence to let him go, but it was clear Terrence wasn't free to do it. He'd mentioned his family earlier, and York could understand how he felt. He wouldn't want to sacrifice his family for a guy he didn't know, either. He hadn't wanted to do what Curt ordered before, but he had, and it had been because of his brother.

He sighed. Everything was a mess. He didn't know how to get out of the situation, or even if he could. There was only one thing he was sure of — Leo would kick his ass if he ever got back to him.

He wanted to. He desperately wanted to leave this house and never think about Curt and the cockatrice shifters again. The problem was that he was stuck, and even though he knew the clan was coming for him, he felt it wouldn't be fast enough. He didn't know what Curt was planning, but it couldn't be good.

A movement at the corner of his eye made him turn. The door was locked, but he was sure he'd seen something poking from it. How was it possible?

"York?" a voice suddenly asked, startling him.

He squinted at the door, trying to understand what he was seeing. A figure appeared, and suddenly, Cooper was standing in front of him.

York's mouth went dry. He'd looked for his brother for so long, had called to him hundreds of times, but right now, he wasn't doing anything that involved Cooper, so how was he here?

Cooper stepped away from the door, rushing to York's side. "What are you doing here? What happened to you?"

York opened his mouth, but he couldn't seem to make it work. What was happening right now?

"York? Are you hurt?" Cooper asked, reaching for York but stopping before touching him.

Of course. He was a ghost, which meant he couldn't touch York without a lot of energy and work, and even then, it wasn't a sure thing.

"You have to tell me you're fine," Cooper begged.

The desperation in his voice finally snapped York out of his shock. "Cooper?" York's voice was tiny.

Cooper smiled. "Yeah. It's me."

York got to his feet. He reached for his brother, then snatched his hand back. "How could you?" he asked.

Cooper seemed surprised by York's anger. "What?"

"You left me!"

Cooper grimaced. "I died, York. I didn't mean to. Trust me. If I could change things, I wouldn't be dead."

"That's not what I was talking about. I've been calling out to you for weeks, trying everything I could to bring you back to me, and you didn't come. Were you here the entire time? Why? What do you have to do with Curt?"

"What do you know about Curt?" Cooper asked, his tone urgent.

"I did everything he asked because he promised he'd bring you back to me."

102

Cooper looked horrified. "What did he have you do? York, you can't have been that stupid. Why did you start working for him?"

York turned around and rubbed his face. He'd imagined his reunion with his brother so many times, but never like this. For a start, he hadn't yelled at his brother when he'd been daydreaming. He should have known he would, though. He was hurt, frustrated, and angry.

He sucked in a breath. Yelling at Cooper wouldn't help anyone, least of all York. He needed to know what was happening and how to get home, and maybe Cooper could help.

"How long have you been here?" he asked.

Cooper looked hesitant. "A while. I didn't know you were involved in any of this. What are you doing here? You said you know Curt?"

York nodded. "I do. A while back, he was looking for psychics. He promised that if I worked for him, he'd help me get you back. I've been trying to pull you to me ever since you died, and it wasn't working." Had Curt known Cooper was here? But he hadn't been allied with the cockatrices until he'd lost that fight against the clan.

Cooper stared at York for a moment before sitting on the edge of the mattress. "Tell me everything that happened to you since I died," he ordered.

York didn't want to. He was ashamed of what he'd done trying to get his brother back. He owed Cooper honesty, though. The clan had forgiven him for what he'd done. Marcel had forgiven him. Surely Cooper could do the same.

So York explained. He told Cooper how alone he'd been after his death, how he'd met the wrong people and had agreed to do things he wasn't proud of. He told him about Marcel and what had happened with him and about the clan that had welcomed him as if he'd always been one of their own. Cooper's expression changed as York spoke, and York had no idea what he was thinking or how he felt.

When he was done explaining, he stopped talking and waited.

Cooper rubbed his face. "I'm so sorry I left you like this. It wasn't my choice."

"I know."

Cooper looked at York. "For a long time, I wasn't sure what had happened to me. I'm pretty sure I didn't even know I was dead. I wandered around, and eventually, I ended up here. I had no idea who the people who lived here were, but then, I found something, or rather, someone."

York frowned. "Who?"

"His name is Valerian. He's a psychic like you, and he's also a prisoner." Cooper hesitated. "The cockatrices and that asshole Curt want to use him. He's not just a psychic but also a mage. He told me that the mix of the two is rare, especially as strong as him. Curt has been trying to convince him to work for him, but Valerian keeps refusing, which is why he's a prisoner. He doesn't have a family that Curt can use against him. He only has me."

York was starting to see where this was going. "He's the reason you didn't come to me when I called for you. You didn't want to leave him." York had been doing it right the entire time. Cooper hadn't appeared because he hadn't wanted to.

"I've been sneaking around the house, trying to find out what was happening and a way to get him out. I had to be careful in the beginning because a woman psychic was working with Curt, but I haven't seen her in a while. From what I know, she's also a mix of psychic and mage but not nearly as powerful as Valerian."

"What does Curt want from him?"

"I don't know, and neither does Valerian. He refuses to talk to Curt, no matter how many times the asshole beats him."

Cooper's gaze drifted along York's face. "He hurt you, too."

"He did, but I'm fine. It's not the first time I've had to deal with him in this kind of situation."

"I hate that you had to go through this. I should have been there for you."

"You didn't choose to die, and even if you'd come to me, I probably would have done something stupid anyway." That wasn't entirely true, but there was no need for Cooper to know.

The only reason York had agreed to work with Curt was to get Cooper back. If Cooper had come to him the first time he'd tried contacting him, neither of them would be here.

But York wouldn't have met Leo. He wouldn't have met the clan. It would have been better for them if he hadn't entered their lives, but it wouldn't have been for him.

He had what he'd always wanted—Cooper was back with him. The problem was that he was stuck.

How was he going to go home?

CHAPTER NINE

It had been days since York had been home. The first day, he'd still had hope the clan would come to get him. Then, he decided that even if the clan didn't, Leo would.

But Leo hadn't come, either.

York was counting the days, but it was starting to be hard to care. He'd been locked in this bedroom for four days now, with his brother coming and going, splitting his time between York and Valerian. York wanted to resent him for not being with him the entire time, but when Cooper talked about Valerian, York could tell how important he was to Cooper. How could he resent that? How could he resent that this Valerian guy was giving Cooper something Cooper had thought he'd lost?

York wasn't sure it was a good idea for Cooper to get in deeper with Valerian, but they didn't seem to have a choice. Valerian was stuck, just like York, and Cooper was his only company. They cared about each other. At the very least, Cooper cared about Valerian. York hadn't met the guy yet, so he couldn't be sure, but he suspected his brother wasn't the only one who had feelings.

That could only end in a disaster. What would happen if they fell in love? Cooper was dead, and there was no changing that. He wouldn't come back to life, and while York was happy to have him in whatever way he could, did the same go for Valerian?

Dammit. York hated not knowing.

The sound of footsteps outside his door told him it was

time for his daily Curt visit. The asshole was coming every day, trying to convince York to work for him. Every time York said no, Curt moved on to threats and beatings, and York's body was more black and blue than pink by now. He didn't think he had anything broken, which was a small miracle, but he couldn't help but wonder how long that would last. Eventually, York would either have to say yes or prepare himself to lose his life. Curt's patience wasn't infinite, and whatever he needed York for, it felt urgent. He didn't need York in particular, just a psychic, and he could no doubt find one elsewhere.

The door creaked as it opened, the sound ominous. York stayed where he was sitting on the bed, but he did turn his attention to the man who walked in. Curt behaved as if he owned the house, and possibly York, too, but York knew that wasn't the case. He'd heard yelling the day after he'd been brought here, so he knew Curt wasn't happy with what the cockatrices were giving him, and they were unhappy with his results. It was a weakness York wanted to exploit, but he wasn't sure how.

"Have you changed your mind yet?" Curt asked.

He sounded almost polite, which frankly was more terrifying than having him scream.

York raised his chin. "I'll never change my mind. You're a cruel asshole, and I don't want anything to do with you."

Curt's expression turned angry. "You'll regret the way you're talking to me."

"I regret even knowing you."

Curt took a step forward. York cringed, knowing what was about to come. Instead of hitting him, Curt stepped in front of the bed and grabbed York's chin. He forced York to look up, his fingers hurting York's chin, but York made sure not to say a word about that. No matter how much pain he was in, he wasn't about to show Curt he was weak.

"You still think your little dragons are coming for you," Curt drawled. "Can't you see it? You're worthless. Why should they come for you when you don't deserve it? They probably think it's for the best that they got rid of you, so you should try getting over it and accept that your future will be with me, not with them."

York swallowed. He'd thought that maybe the clan had decided he wasn't worth it, but that was the darkest part of his personality talking. Since he'd lost Cooper, he felt like he didn't matter to anyone, even though he knew that wasn't the case. The dragons would come for him. It was just more complicated than he'd expected. He'd be surprised if they even knew where he was because even though they'd suspected Curt was working with the cockatrices, their territory was vast. It would take a while for the clan to locate York's position, then to get to him, and they were risking a war to do so.

York glared at Curt. "Nothing you can say will change my mind."

Curt pushed York's face away. "You'll regret that."

York had no doubt he would. Curt would make sure he was in as much pain as possible without killing him.

York expected the punch coming his way. He tried shielding himself, but it was no use, and when it hit, he whimpered and fell back. Thankfully, he was on the bed, so Curt couldn't kick him. Curt's hands were more than enough to do damage, though.

This time, it went on for so long that York wondered if Curt was going to kill him. He thought maybe so, because his entire body hurt, and by the time Curt was done, he was breathing hard. Hurting York took a lot of energy, but that didn't seem to be a problem for Curt.

"You'll change your mind," Curt promised as he left.

York tried breathing through the pain while Curt left. He didn't relax immediately, knowing Curt might come back, but after a few minutes, he felt safe.

That was when the sob broke out of his throat. He tried to keep it in, but it was useless, so he grabbed the pillow and pressed it against his face, screaming against it. It hurt, but at least that way, Curt wouldn't hear him cry.

"I'll kill him," Cooper said, startling York.

York blinked up at him. The pillow he'd used was streaked with blood, but he didn't care. It wasn't his stuff, anyway, so he used the sheet he'd been sleeping on to mop off the blood, sweat, and drool from his face.

Cooper was pacing on the other side of the room, still muttering about hurting Curt.

"I don't know if you noticed, but you're dead. You won't be able to hurt him," York pointed out. He should go to the bathroom to clean up, but he didn't have the energy right now.

Cooper turned to face him. His lips were pressed so hard together that they were white, and he tightened his hands into fists as if he wanted to go after Curt. York had no doubt he did, but there wasn't anything he could do, unfortunately.

"I'll help you escape," Cooper said.

"That would be great, but what about Valerian?"

Cooper bit his lower lip and looked away. "I can't leave him."

York wasn't surprised. Considering he was pretty sure his brother was half in love with Valerian—if not completely—he'd expected it. "I want to help him, too. It's not right that he's stuck here with Curt."

"I don't know if you'll have time to free him."

"I'll find it. I promise. And if I can't take him with me right away, I'll return with the clan. I don't want to leave anyone behind, especially not someone who's important to you."

Cooper was still hesitant. York didn't blame him, but they had to do something. He wasn't the only one in danger. If

Curt was so eager to hurt York, what was he doing to Valerian?

"I know we haven't spent time together since you died and that I did horrible things. I promise I'll keep Valerian as safe as I can," he said. "The only reason I hurt Marcel was because I wanted you back. I have you now, and since Valerian is important to you, he's important to me."

Cooper nodded. "I'll stay with him until you come back."

"Why? I promise we'll come back for him." York didn't want to leave Cooper behind. He didn't know if he could survive losing his brother again.

Cooper seemed to know what was going through York's mind, and he moved closer. They couldn't touch, but having Cooper's hand hover over York's cheek was almost as good. "I believe you, but I can't leave him behind. Besides, I'm already dead. Curt can't hurt me."

But York wondered if that was true. Curt had used ghosts before and hadn't cared what they wanted or felt. If he found out Cooper was helping Valerian and York, he'd make sure Cooper couldn't do so again.

Leo leaned forward, examining the map they now had of cockatrice territory.

It had taken them a few days and several trips for Tim's grandfather, but now, they knew where they were going.

Working with a ghost definitely had its upsides.

Leo couldn't see Kenneth, but Victor had been talking with the ghost. It had been Victor's idea and the only reason Leo had agreed to wait and not do something stupid like barge into cockatrice territory without knowing where he was going. Victor and Kenneth had put together a map of where most of the houses were, where the alpha lived, and, more importantly, where York was being kept.

"And you're sure Curt isn't staying there with York?" Victor asked the empty space next to him.

It was odd to be part of the conversation when Leo couldn't see one of the participants, so he looked away. Tim was standing next to him, and he winked as they waited for Victor to have his answer.

Victor finally turned to them. They were all gathered around the long table in the conference room, and everyone seemed excited to go to the rescue, even Jerome, although Leo suspected that was more because he wanted to kick ass. Elijah had been clear that the psychics would have to stay behind, but the dragons were welcome to help as long as they planned everything down to every second. He'd tried keeping Leo behind, but there was no way Leo could let the others go in to rescue York and not go with them.

"He says Curt has been coming and going, but he's not staying at the house with York. Only one cockatrice shifter is, and he's not as bad as Curt. He hasn't hit York, at the very least."

Leo saw red and had to take a deep breath so he wouldn't snap. "He's been hurting York?" he asked.

Victor grimaced. "He's been beating him. I'm sorry." He cocked his head, probably listening to Kenneth. "Kenneth says there's another man and a ghost there. The ghost seems friendly with York and the other man, but Kenneth didn't dare try talking to him."

"We don't want the cockatrices to know we're coming," Elijah intervened.

"Kenneth says that Curt is never there during the night. He spends that time with the cockatrice alpha."

Elijah nodded. "Considering he's hurting York, we should go tonight."

Leo could have kissed him. He wanted to go right away, and while he understood why Elijah had nixed that idea, he needed to do something. York was in danger, and that didn't sit right with Leo and his dragon. He wanted to hunt Curt and kill him, but Elijah had warned him to stay away. They weren't ready to deal with Curt and the cockatrices yet, but they would be eventually. For tonight, Leo's focus would be on York. He could get revenge later when Curt least expected it.

There were still many details to deal with, but Leo didn't have the patience to focus on them. He started pacing, looking out the window every time he walked past one of them. He knew he had to be annoying, but no one said anything until Marcel stepped in front of him and grabbed his shoulder.

"We'll find him," he promised.

"I know. In what state will he be, though? You heard Victor. That asshole is beating him, and considering what he did to Marcel, he won't hesitate to hurt York."

"I know. We'll do everything we can and give York the care he needs, but we have to focus on getting him back now. Once we have him, we can do everything else."

He was right, but it was hard not to think of York all alone in that house, being hurt day in and day out. This time, he wasn't giving Curt what he wanted, and Curt was a cruel asshole. Leo had no doubt that was why he was beating York. He was trying to make him say yes to whatever he needed, and York was being stubborn and not giving in.

The one time he should have, and he kept saying no. He and Leo would need to have a chat once he was home.

Marcel stayed with Leo the entire time, up until they were finally ready to leave the house. Elijah wouldn't be coming with them, but he didn't need to. They were sneaking in, not attacking the cockatrices. Between Jerome, Marcel, Tim, and Leo, there were more than enough dragons to manage that. Victor was coming along so they could continue to communicate with Kenneth, and they all had their cell phones in case something happened.

They piled into Jerome's car, and Leo started bouncing his leg. He couldn't stay still, his thoughts entirely on York.

He had no idea what they'd find once they reached cockatrice territory, but he could imagine, unfortunately. If Curt had been beating up York, York wouldn't be in great shape. Thinking of that made Leo want to rampage, so he took a deep breath, then another, and forced himself to calm down.

Eventually, he and York would get their revenge. They'd make sure Curt couldn't hurt anyone ever again. For now, Leo would focus on what was truly important.

Getting York back.

Victor continued explaining what Kenneth was saying until they reached cockatrice territory. They'd memorized the map so they knew where they were going and where to leave the car. Victor would stay hidden, so Jerome, Marcel, and Leo gave him a moment with Tim. Leo could only imagine what it felt like for Victor. Tim was going into a dangerous situation, but it was for a good cause. Victor hadn't tried to stop him when he'd volunteered, but it couldn't be easy. Shit, it had to be *terrifying.* The thought of losing York made Leo want to scream and cry at the same time, and they'd just recently gotten together.

"Ready?" Tim asked when he reached them.

They looked at each other and nodded.

"Ready," Leo confirmed.

They snuck into cockatrice territory without a hitch. Kenneth had warned them about the guards, so they knew where they were located, as well as that there weren't many of them around. The cockatrices clearly didn't think anyone would attack them, and they were right. Leo and the others weren't here to attack. They were here to rescue, at least this time around.

Instead of attacking the cockatrice guards the way Leo

wanted, they snuck past them and deeper into cockatrice territory. They had to stop a few times to get their bearings, but Marcel was in charge, and he knew where they were going. Leo trusted him implicitly, and he had no problem following him.

He'd follow Marcel to the depths of hell if it meant getting York back.

York couldn't continue saying no to his brother. As much as he wanted Cooper to come along, Cooper wouldn't get hurt even if he stayed back. He'd also support Valerian, and considering how important that seemed to be to him, York couldn't find it in himself to continue insisting.

He sighed and peered at his reflection in the chipped mirror in the bathroom. "I think that the sooner you can get me out of here, the better it will be."

"That's what I've been telling you all along," Cooper snapped. He sucked in a breath and pinched the bridge of his nose. "I'm sorry. I'm just worried about you and Valerian, and I feel powerless. I can't do anything to help either of you."

"That's not true. You're helping me escape, and you'll eventually help Valerian. I'm sure he'll be grateful."

"He thinks I'm an idiot because I'm not going with you."

York arched a brow, then stopped because it fucking hurt. "You've talked about this?"

"Yeah. He told me I should go with you, and I said I wasn't leaving him. That's when he said I was an idiot and that I'd been talking about you for ages, and now that I had you back, I needed to do the right thing."

York didn't know Valerian, but he suspected he'd like him a lot once they met. "Well, I won't say he's wrong, but I understand why you want to stay. He needs you."

Cooper nodded. "Exactly. Besides, you told me you had an

entire clan waiting for you. You have people out there. He doesn't have anyone but me."

That was kind of sad, and York found himself feeling happy that Valerian had Cooper. "As long as you swear that you'll come to me the next time I call you. It could be important, and it could be about Valerian's rescue." York wished there was more he could do for Valerian, but he was only one man, and not in the best of shape. His entire body hurt, and he was still bleeding from his puffy lower lip.

"I swear I will. Valerian wanted me to go to you before, but I wasn't willing to leave him alone. There's not much I can do when Curt threatens and hits him, but I can be there for him and comfort him."

"I'm sure he's happy you stayed, even though he won't say it." York straightened. "All right. What do we do?"

Cooper grinned, happy that York was finally getting out of there. York felt the same way, so he didn't blame his brother.

"I'll go outside. You need to pick the lock."

York swallowed and stared at the door. "I'm not sure I can."

"Well, there's nothing I can do about it. I can tell you if someone's coming, but I can't touch anything." He hesitated, then shook his head. "I'm sorry."

"It's fine. It's just hard to remember you're a ghost sometimes."

Cooper grinned. "Tell me about it."

York laughed, but they didn't have time to waste. As soon as Cooper snuck out through the door, he turned his attention to the lock.

He'd done things he wasn't proud of during his time with Curt. Curt wasn't a good person, and it wasn't like he'd paid York and the others for their work. York had needed to find food and survive, which meant that sometimes, he'd stolen. He'd also picked a few locks, and he hoped he'd be able to do it with this one, too.

Luck was on his side. This was a normal home lock, and it didn't take much for York to break through it. Thankfully, Terrence hadn't noticed York had kept one of the forks that had come with his meal, or maybe he had but hadn't said anything. York suspected Terrence wanted out of this situation but couldn't do anything about it because of his family. He couldn't help York outright, but there were a few things he'd done that made York believe that if it weren't for his family, York would already be free.

The door creaked as it opened, and York held his breath. When nothing happened, he pushed it open wider and peeked out into the hallway.

Cooper was there, and he grinned at him. "You did it."

York nodded. No one else could hear Cooper, but Terrence would be able to hear York, and he didn't want to risk it.

Cooper seemed to understand, because he nodded and gestured at York to follow him. York was as silent as he could manage, only pausing next to the door behind which Valerian was kept. He was stuck, and York couldn't do anything to help him. He hated feeling useless, but there wasn't anything he could do for Valerian on his own and in the state that he was in.

Luckily he wasn't supposed to know about the other man. He only did because of Cooper, so Curt probably wouldn't think about moving him. That meant that when York returned with the clan, Valerian would probably still be there, and he'd be waiting for them. Thanks to Cooper, he knew help was coming.

York followed Cooper downstairs, then through the house until they reached the back door. It was in the kitchen, and while the air smelled of food, it was empty.

"Terrence?" York asked in a whisper.

Cooper shook his head. "He's not here. I don't know where

he is in the house, but I couldn't find him anywhere. That's how I knew it was time for you to go."

York swallowed. He knew he'd see Cooper again, but this felt too much like a goodbye. "I'll see you soon," he whispered.

Cooper reached for him, but he couldn't touch him. "Yes," he promised. "I stayed back for Valerian, but now that I know you'll help, I won't resist your calls anymore. I shouldn't have to begin with.

"Valerian was right."

"He was. He's too smart for his own good."

York wanted to cry and laugh at the same time. He wanted to hug Cooper, to tell him everything would be okay, but he needed to go.

He reached for the door, turning the handle.

"Wait," Cooper said. "I'll see if there's anyone outside."

But it was too late. York had already started opening the door, and someone was standing just outside of it.

CHAPTER TEN

They'd almost done it. They were at the back door, ready to sneak in, when it opened. There was nowhere for Leo to hide, so he braced himself, ready to attack whoever was coming out of the house.

It was York.

The two of them froze, staring at each other. Leo wanted nothing more than to pull York into his arms, but even in the darkness, he could see the bruises on his skin. York had been too thin before, but it had gotten worse, as if he'd lost weight during the four days he'd spent with Curt. Kenneth had said that Curt was feeding York, but seeing him, Leo wasn't sure. Either that, or York had refused to eat the food, which might make sense.

Tim's shoulder bumped against Leo's as he rushed toward York. York never stopped staring at Leo, even when Tim pulled him into his arms. Leo could finally move, so he stepped forward, and as soon as Tim was done, Leo dragged York closer.

"We need to go," Jerome snapped. He kept looking around, clearly expecting the cockatrices to find them.

"What happened? How did you escape?" Leo asked.

York shook his head. "There's no time. We have to go."

He was right, of course. He could answer their questions at home, but the first thing they needed to do was to leave cockatrice territory.

Leo wrapped an arm around York's shoulders and pulled him forward. He peered into the house, but no one was there, and he quickly closed the door of the kitchen York had come out of.

But York didn't come easily. He looked back, his movements slow. Leo worried that he was in too much pain to walk. Kenneth hadn't been kidding when he'd said that Curt was beating up York.

"Do we have time to go back?" York asked.

"The car isn't far. We'll make it," Leo promised.

York shook his head. "I meant inside the house. There's someone else there, and I promised we'd help him."

Leo and Marcel looked at each other. It would be dangerous to come back, but it would be just as dangerous to linger. "Who is that person?"

"A friend."

That was hard to believe because, as far as Leo was aware, York hadn't had any friends before reaching the clan.

"Considering the state you're in, I don't think that's a good idea," Jerome said. "If you need to help whoever is here, I'm sure Elijah will be all right with sending someone else now that we know how to get into cockatrice territory."

York's eyes were wide. "But they'll expect you."

"Why should they? We don't know who that person is. You're a clan member, but he's not, so why should we come back for them?"

York looked hurt. "Because they don't deserve to be stuck here."

"I never said they did. That's what the cockatrices are going to think, though. We need to get you home, where you can get the rest and care you need. I promise I won't abandon this person, and neither will the clan."

Was Leo in an alternate universe where Jerome cared about what York wanted? Because this wasn't like him. What he was saying didn't make sense, at least not coming from his lips.

But it helped York relax, and he finally started moving. He stared back one last time, and Leo could have sworn he heard him whisper that he promised he wouldn't leave Valerian here. Who was he talking to? Was that ghost Kenneth had mentioned around? It was the most probable explanation, and Leo couldn't wait for York to explain what had happened while he'd been here. It seemed he'd gone through a lot, and not just physically.

"If we're lucky, we'll get back to the car without anyone noticing us," Tim whispered.

Of course, that was when everything went to shit. Leo noticed York was crying and started to ask what was going on, but before he could, someone yelled. It wasn't any of them, which meant they'd been found.

Leo swore. They had to get out of here, dammit. How were they supposed to do that with the cockatrices after them?

He sucked in a breath and tried to calm down.

They had a plan for this, too. He had to remember that. Elijah had known something like this might happen, and he'd planned accordingly. This wasn't anything they weren't ready for, and York being with them wouldn't change that.

Marcel and Leo exchanged a glance. Marcel nodded, tilting his chin toward York. "Stay with him."

"How many?"

"I don't know, but I'd say a few. More will come if we don't get out of here soon, though."

"Then let's do it."

A group of three cockatrice shifters burst from between the trees, their footsteps making it sound like they were a herd of elephants. Leo placed himself in front of York, who was sobbing but trying to stop. He'd pressed a hand against his mouth and was sucking in deep breaths, but it wasn't working very well. Leo wanted nothing more than to comfort him, but he needed to focus on keeping him safe first.

Luckily, they weren't alone. Jerome, Marcel, and Tim stepped up, facing the three cockatrices who'd found them. Leo could hear more footsteps behind them, though, so he knew he'd have to fight, too.

"Will you be fine here?" he asked York.

"Where are you going?"

"Nowhere, but I need to do something. More cockatrices are coming."

"Curt?"

"I don't know. We'll get you out of here, though. I promise."

"I trust you."

With the trees around them, it would be better if they didn't shift. It was a pity because it would be much easier to take care of the cockatrices in their dragon form, even though they'd have to risk the cockatrices shifting, too. It was a risk Jerome had been willing to take, but Leo had agreed with Marcel and Tim that it would be too dangerous. One-on-one, the dragons would probably win against the cockatrices. With more cockatrices present, though, they could swarm the dragons, and then they wouldn't make it out alive. Besides, it would be better if they managed to keep who they were a secret from the cockatrices. Leo doubted that would work, considering they were taking York, but Elijah had given them an order, and he'd follow it as long as it didn't put anyone in danger.

More cockatrices burst through the trees, and Leo faced them. Luckily, there were only an additional two, and one went straight for Jerome, maybe because he was kind of short. Leo would never dare tease him about that, and he knew Jerome was a fierce fighter. How tall he was didn't change that.

The other cockatrice threw himself at Leo. Leo blinked, wondering what the cockatrice was doing because it was clear the guy didn't have any idea how to fight. That was better for

Leo, so he wasn't about to protest.

He grabbed the guy's fist when the guy aimed at his face and pushed him away. The guy stumbled back, but unfortunately, he didn't stop moving, and the next punch he threw landed squarely on Leo's jaw.

Leo stumbled back and grinned. He'd hoped they wouldn't have to fight, but since they were being forced to, he'd make the most out of it. He wanted revenge for what the cockatrices had done to York.

The problem was that more cockatrice shifters kept appearing. Leo managed to put down most of them, but he wouldn't be able to keep up for much longer. He was grateful when York clocked one of them on the back of the head with a branch, and he turned toward his boyfriend, making sure he was all right. When York's eyes widened, Leo knew something bad was happening behind him. He steeled himself, expecting to feel pain, but nothing happened. He turned around to find a man flat on his face on the ground and a branch floating in the air.

He stared at it for only a few seconds before it tumbled down in the dirt. "What the fuck?" he asked no one in particular. That had to have been a ghost, right? Had York spent his entire time with the cockatrices chatting with that ghost and making friends with him?

Leo had questions but no time to ask them because another cockatrice took the place of the one on the ground, and the fight was on again.

York had been horrified when that man had stepped behind Leo to attack him. He'd opened his mouth to tell Leo, but he'd known he wouldn't be in time. Luckily, Cooper had been hovering around since York had left the house, and he'd stepped in. York didn't understand how his brother had been able to pick up the branch and hit the cockatrice shifter without a boost of energy, but whatever had happened, he was grateful.

"Thank you," he said as he pressed his back against the closest tree. He felt useless, but even if he'd been healthy, he doubted he'd have been able to do much when it came to this fight.

Cooper hovered close. "Are you all right? You look like you're about to faint."

York felt like he was, but he forced himself to smile. "I guess I'm more tired than I expected."

"Daily beatings and almost no food will do that to you." Cooper looked from the fight to the house.

York knew Cooper wanted to go back to Valerian, but for now, Valerian was fine. He was locked in his bedroom, and he'd stay there, hopefully. York prayed Curt wouldn't think of moving him, but even if he did, York and the clan would find their way to him. Now that Cooper knew York was going to help, he'd promised to come when York pulled him.

Leo suddenly grabbed York's hand and dragged him forward. York stumbled, but he went, surprised to see all the cockatrice shifters were either unconscious or moaning in pain. Leo and the others were rushing forward, which meant they had a narrow window of time to get away. York had to go with them, but he couldn't help looking back. He felt like he was losing his brother again, and he didn't think he'd be strong enough to heal if he never saw Cooper again after tonight.

"I need to go back," Cooper said, coming after York. "You'll be safe. Your clan has you."

York kept moving, but he was doing so while also looking back at his brother. "I swear we'll come back."

"I know. I have faith in you, York. I trust you."

The tears were coming down again, but York didn't try to stop them. It would be useless when he'd start crying again in seconds, anyway.

Cooper stopped moving and hovered there, staring back at York. York looked at him for as long as he could until he disappeared between the trees. He was sobbing, unable to see where he was putting his feet, especially in the darkness. He wasn't worried, though, because Leo hooked an arm around his shoulders and held him close as he guided him out of the woods where cockatrice territory was.

"What happened? Are you hurt?" Leo asked urgently.

York shook his head, then nodded. "Nothing a few days of rest won't heal," he promised.

"You're crying."

York wiped his cheeks, but he wasn't sure how much good it did. "I'll be fine." He wasn't sure he could say anything else right now.

Leo clearly wanted to push, but instead, he nodded and kept guiding York. York wasn't sure how long they walked, but it couldn't have been much longer. Then a car appeared in front of them. He sucked in a breath, hoping it meant they were about to go home, almost crying when Kenneth appeared.

York knew him. He'd seen him around the clan house, and Kenneth was kind and gentle. He'd told York he was Tim's grandfather, and York felt it meant he could trust him.

"It's good to see you in one piece," Kenneth said.

"It's good to be in one piece," York told him as the driver's door opened, and Victor stumbled out.

He made a beeline for Tim, while Leo and Marcel guided York into the car. He was so tired he felt like he could fall asleep in seconds. He had no doubt everyone had questions, but he hoped they wouldn't ask them in the car. Maybe he could sleep for a bit, at least until they reached the clan.

York briefly wondered how they'd all fit into the car, which wasn't that big. He understood when Leo climbed in, then pulled him into his lap. He settled in the middle of the back seat, with Marcel on one side and Tim on the other. Jerome was driving, and Victor was in the passenger seat next to him.

It was probably dangerous in case they had an accident or something like that, but York couldn't find it in himself to care. He leaned against Leo and closed his eyes, breathing in Leo's scent and reminding himself that he was safe. He was in pain, both physically and mentally, but he'd be fine.

The silence in the car was tense as Jerome drove them away. York didn't understand why until he realized they were still in cockatrice territory. He hoped the cockatrices weren't coming after them, but he couldn't be sure, and he felt incredibly guilty at the thought that he was once again putting the clan in danger. He wasn't surprised they'd come for him, since they kept telling him he was a clan member, but he almost wished they hadn't.

Eventually, the tension in the car dissipated. York understood it was because they left cockatrice territory, and he allowed himself to fully relax. His eyelids were heavy, probably because he'd barely slept in the past four days, and he finally felt safe and warm. Tim had found a blanket somewhere and awkwardly wrapped it around York's shoulders. Leo hadn't let go of York even for a moment, and Marcel had gently teased him about it.

Now that they were far enough away from cockatrice territory, everyone's attention turned to York. He wondered if he could fake sleep, but he felt he owed everyone in the car an explanation. They'd come to his rescue, even Jerome, who was the last person York had expected to be there.

"How are you doing?" Marcel asked gently.

"Well, I feel like I've been in a fight with a truck and lost, but I'll be okay."

Leo's entire body tensed. "I'll kill him," he promised.

"I won't say no to that offer, but you can't go back for

now."

"I know. We'll have to eventually, though, right? You said there was someone else who needed to be rescued?"

"Yeah. Did Kenneth tell you about him?" Because why else would Kenneth be there? He had to have spied on Curt to be able to tell the people in the car when and where to go in.

"He mentioned that someone else was kept prisoner and that a ghost was hanging around."

York's eyes prickled with tears again. He felt like a wet blanket, and he buried deeper against Leo. "He's right. There was another ghost."

"Is he why you're crying?"

York nodded. "I didn't expect having to be kidnapped to see my brother again."

Leo sucked in a breath. "Cooper was there?"

"Yeah. He attached himself to this other guy, Valerian. They became friends, and Cooper stayed back with him. I promised him we'd come back for Valerian." York tried to sit up. "I can't leave Cooper there. I know he's a ghost, but it doesn't mean Curt can't hurt him, and he won't come back to me if we don't help Valerian."

"Why don't you get some rest and wait to explain this to everyone?" Marcel gently suggested. "That way, you'll only have to do it once."

It was clear from Leo's expression that he wanted to push, but eventually, he nodded. "Marcel is right. Get some sleep. This can wait until we're home."

York was glad. His eyes burned from tears and exhaustion, and he wanted nothing more than to close them, even if it was only for half an hour. He'd have to deal with reality soon enough, and he wanted to take advantage of the fact that he was safe in Leo's arms, at least for a little while. Reality wasn't going anywhere. It would still be there once they arrived home and York had to face it. For now, he sighed in pleasure and allowed his eyes to slide closed.

Even though they'd long left cockatrice territory, Leo stayed tense until they got home. He breathed easier once they were behind the gate, and he looked down at York, smiling a bit when he saw that his boyfriend was asleep against him. The smile turned into a scowl when, after Jerome parked the car, Tim opened his door, and the light illuminated the bruises on York's face.

Leo was going to kill Curt if it was the last thing he did.

Leo kissed York's forehead, trying to wake him up gently. He thought it worked for a moment, and York blinked his eyes open. Then, he jerked away, and he would have fallen off Leo's lap if they hadn't been stuck in the car the way they were. York wasn't afraid of him, but Leo wasn't sure how to react. Should he try comforting him, or should he give him space?

Thankfully, he didn't have to worry for long. York stared at him for a moment, his gaze unfocused. Then, he relaxed, and Leo knew his boyfriend had recognized him.

"We stopped," York said.

"We're home. We should go upstairs. You can shower and eat something, then go to bed."

York nodded. "I feel I haven't had a good night's sleep in forever."

Not forever, but certainly the four days he'd been away from the clan. Once again, Leo felt the need to find Curt and torture him to death, but instead, he decided to focus on York. He helped him out of the car, grinning when he saw the crowd of people waiting for them by the front door. He could see his parents, but also Marcel's and Tim's. Victor's brothers were there, along with Lindsey and Will. They were waiting, maybe because they didn't want to crowd York, and Elijah was the first step forward.

Leo was relieved to see Albert behind Elijah. He was a doctor, so he'd be able to tell whether or not York needed to go to the hospital. Leo hoped the answer to that would be no, but what did he know? He just wanted York to be healthy, which clearly wasn't the case.

"It's so good to see you," Elijah told York when he reached the car.

York was leaning against Leo, clearly exhausted, but he smiled. "It's good to be home. Thank you for sending people to get me back."

"We couldn't abandon you."

"Even though it was my fault I got captured?"

Elijah smiled. "I won't say it wasn't a stupid thing to do, but your heart was in the right place. Can you just promise you won't do something like that again? I don't think our hearts can take it."

York chuckled, then winced and pressed a hand to his side. "I don't think I want to leave the house for a while."

"Well, you have the yard if you need some fresh air. I don't know if you remember Albert, but he's a doctor, and he agreed to examine you to make sure you don't need to go to the hospital."

York grimaced. "It would be great if I could avoid that. I just want to go to bed and sleep for a week."

"Can you tell me what happened?" Albert asked gently.

Leo huffed. This wasn't the right time or place to do this, and he wished Albert and Elijah could see that.

"Maybe we should go inside," he said.

"Of course," Albert agreed readily. "It would be more comfortable for York."

"York will explain everything tomorrow," Leo declared, looking around. "Right now, he needs food and rest."

"As long as we know he's okay, I think we can all wait until tomorrow," Elijah agreed.

"But my brother," York started to protest.

"There's nothing we can do for him and Valerian right now," Leo told him. "They'll be fine until tomorrow. Besides, we can't go out there again tonight."

York looked like he wanted to protest, but instead, he nodded. He had to realize that Leo was right, and Leo was thankful for that. He didn't want to have to fight with York and lock him in his bedroom.

Because that was where he led York as soon as they were inside. Maybe York would prefer to go to his own bedroom, but Leo didn't think he could let go of him so soon after rescuing him. He needed to reassure himself that York was all right and safe, which wouldn't happen if York slept in his own bed. If that was what he wanted, Leo would sleep in front of his door.

But York didn't say anything when Leo walked him to his bedroom and ushered him inside. Albert went straight to work, guiding York to the bathroom. Leo wanted to go with them, but Elijah stopped him with a hand on the shoulder.

"Give them space. Albert will tell us if something is wrong and we need to take York to the hospital."

Leo sighed. "I don't know if I can stay away from him."

"You're freaking out over what happened."

"Wouldn't you in my place?"

Elijah's expression turned pensive. "I suppose I would if someone I loved had been in York's place. How did it go? And what's that about York's brother?"

Leo didn't have the energy to explain right now, but he had nothing better to do while Albert and York were in the bathroom. "Turns out the ghost Kenneth saw was York's brother, Cooper."

"The Cooper he's tried contacting since he arrived here?"

"Yeah. I don't have many details, but apparently, he was

there because of the other guy Curt is keeping locked up."

Elijah pinched the bridge of his nose. "What is it with that asshole and keeping people prisoner?"

"I don't know, but I'm pretty sure York promised his brother he'd get Valerian out, and he won't want to go back on that promise."

"He won't have to."

"Even though Valerian isn't a clan member?" Hell, they didn't know anything about Valerian except for his name and the fact that he was a guy.

"It wouldn't sit well with me to leave someone in Curt's clutches, no matter who they are. Besides, if Curt went through the trouble of grabbing this guy and keeping him, it means he thinks he can use him. It would be better to take Valerian away from him so we can stop whatever he's planning."

Leo couldn't say he disagreed. "I'll tell York once he leaves the bathroom. He'll be happy to know you're eager to help."

"Tell him that and that everyone here is happy to have him back. Hopefully, he'll finally feel like part of the clan now that we rescued him."

"I don't know about that, but I'll do my best to convince him. Thank you, Elijah."

Elijah patted Leo's shoulder. "Don't worry about it. Take care of him, and I'll see you both tomorrow. I hate that York will have to relive what he's gone through, but there's no way out of it, unfortunately."

Leo wished York didn't have to think about his time with Curt ever again, but Elijah was right. They needed to know what had happened and what they were going against.

Elijah left as Tim came in. Leo would have sent him away if he hadn't been carrying a tray full of food, and as it was, he almost kissed him. Tim grinned like an asshole as he put the tray down on the dresser.

"I knew he'd be hungry." His smile dimmed. "How is he?"

"I don't know. Albert is in the bathroom with him. I'll let everyone know as soon as he comes out, but I don't think York will be up to talking to anyone until tomorrow."

Tim raised his hands. "I'm not here to talk to him. I'm just happy he's okay, and I wanted him to have food. Text us so we know he's fine, and we'll see both of you tomorrow."

Leo was relieved Tim wasn't trying to stick around, and even more so when Albert finally left the bathroom about fifteen minutes later and confirmed that York would be okay.

"He has a lot of bruises, and he's in pain, but nothing's broken. It looks like the man who did this knew what he was doing."

Albert's expression told Leo what he thought of Curt. Leo shared that feeling, and he was pretty sure that if Albert had been a different kind of guy, he'd have demanded Curt pay for what he'd done.

"Is there anything I need to do?" Leo asked.

Albert held out a tub of cream. "Put this on his bruises. I already gave him painkillers, but he wanted to shower, so I haven't put any of this on him. Make sure he eats, drinks water, and gets some rest. I know enough of the situation to be aware of the fact that it's far from over."

Unfortunately, he was right. Even with York away from Curt, Curt was still a danger, especially with this Valerian guy with him. Leo had no idea what Valerian could do, but he suspected it wouldn't be good for anyone involved. That meant they had to get him away from Curt, and soon.

But not tonight. Tonight, Leo would take care of York, which was what he did once York left the bathroom. He made sure York ate, slathered him in cream, getting angrier every time he saw another bruise, then put him to bed. York fell asleep as soon as his head hit the pillow, but it took Leo a long time to do the same.

CHAPTER ELEVEN

When Leo woke up, the first thing he did was look for York. Luckily, he didn't have to look long or far, because York was snuggled against his side, holding on to him with an arm and a leg. He was plastered against Leo's side, and that was all Leo had ever wanted from life.

He relaxed, not wanting to wake up York. He needed his rest after what had happened to him, and he wouldn't have long. Eventually, they'd have to go downstairs and face everyone who wanted to see York and talk to him, but for now, they were in a peaceful bubble, and Leo didn't want it to pop.

He did have to use the bathroom, though, so he pushed a pillow between him and York and extricated himself from York's arms. York smacked his lips and burrowed his face against the pillow. It was adorable, even with the bruises marring his face.

Thinking about those and how they'd come to be made Leo want to rampage, or at the very least to find Curt and introduce him to his fist.

Leo sucked in a breath, breathed in and out a few times, and told himself to calm down. He wouldn't help York by freaking out every time he saw him. York needed to feel loved and not like Leo couldn't even look at him without getting angry. That was a Leo problem, not a York problem, and Leo had to be there for York.

He took his time in the bathroom, waiting until he was sure he was as calm as he could get to return to the bedroom. He brushed his teeth and washed up, giving himself time,

132

relieved to see that once he was done, York was still asleep. He'd turned away from the window, maybe because the sun was rising higher, and was buried in a nest of pillows and blankets. He looked like he belonged, and Leo wanted him to. He didn't want York to move back to his bedroom. It had been a safe place for York when he'd first arrived here, a refuge, but he didn't need it anymore.

Or at least, Leo hoped so.

He slid back into bed, grimacing when York's eyes fluttered open. "Sorry. I didn't mean to wake you up."

York gave Leo a sleepy smile and moved closer. He tilted his head up to kiss Leo but stopped before their lips could touch. "I need to brush my teeth," he muttered.

He was out of bed before Leo could tell him he didn't need to. Leo didn't care if York had morning breath. He just wanted him in his arms.

Luckily, York was faster in the bathroom than Leo had been. When he came out, still wearing Leo's too-big t-shirt and shorts he'd borrowed last night, his face was still damp, and his breath smelled of mint. He hesitated when he reached the bed, but Leo would have none of that, and he lifted the blankets to show him he was welcome.

York's smile was like the sun, even with the split lip. He scrambled into bed and took his place by Leo's side again. Leo hadn't put his t-shirt back on after washing up, but York didn't seem to have a problem with that. He ran his fingertips up and down Leo's chest and stomach, looking and feeling utterly relaxed. That was enough for Leo to know York's place was in his bed and life.

"How are you feeling?" he asked, keeping his voice soft. He didn't want to break the moment.

"Like I was in a fight and lost, but it was good to wake up next to you."

"It was." Leo was pretty sure it was too soon, but York had

a history of not feeling loved or needed. "I'd like to wake up next to you every day for the rest of my life."

York turned wide eyes to Leo. "You would?"

Leo wiggled down until he and York were both on their sides, looking at each other. York's cheeks were flushed, and he was trying hard to look at Leo, but his gaze kept skittering away. He was nervous now, and while Leo disliked that he'd made York feel that way, he pushed ahead. He suspected that was the only way to make York feel better.

"I want nothing more than to make you happy," he said, pouring his heart out in a way he never had. He trusted York to take care of his heart, though. "I don't know when it happened exactly, but I'm in love with you. I went from not being sure I could trust you and being wary of you for what you did to Marcel to falling so completely in love with you that I can't imagine a life without you. When you were with Curt, I thought I'd go nuts. I never want you to go through something like that again. I want to take care of you, be there for you, and love you. I don't see a reason for us to stay in separate bedrooms when I plan for us to share a bed every night, anyway, but of course, if you need your space—"

York surged forward to kiss Leo. Leo supposed it meant yes, although he'd make sure to ask.

Later, though.

Leo pushed his hands under York's t-shirt. He needed more skin, but he took care of being gentle. He hadn't seen York without his clothes on since last night, but he imagined the bruises were now blooming all over his skin.

York reacted in a way Leo hadn't expected. He scrambled to his knees, pushing the blankets away and yanking his shirt off. There wasn't any hesitation in the way he moved, although he did wince when he raised his arms.

Leo understood why as soon as he looked at York's naked chest. It was as black and blue as his face, with one long bruise going from York's left pectoral to his hip and one on his right side that looked suspiciously like a boot print. The pain or the way he looked didn't stop him, though. Once he threw his t-shirt away, he scrambled to push his shorts off, and Leo decided that since York was getting naked, he should, too.

Leo pushed his pajama pants down but tangled his legs in the blankets. He scowled at them and sat up to free himself, leaning forward. Two arms circled around his waist, stroking the skin just above his groin as a very naked York plastered himself against Leo's back.

"No underwear?" York murmured.

"You didn't wear them, either."

Leo shuddered at how throaty York's voice was. The feeling of York's fingers brushing his skin, going lower and lower as Leo freed himself and leaned back against York's chest, and what he was sure was the damp head of York's cock pressing against his back, made Leo's cock grow harder. York's hand slid lower, circling around the base, stroking along his length.

Leo hadn't expected any of this. York had always been timid and hesitant, even the first time they'd been together. Maybe it was because of what he'd been through with Curt and knowing he could have lost all of this, or maybe it was because he felt more secure in his position with the clan and Leo, but York seemed to be coming out of his shell, and Leo loved it.

He stood up, dislodging York from his back even though it meant not feeling him for a bit. It wouldn't last long, thankfully. He finally got free from the sheets, pushed off his pajama pants, and kicked them off. Then, he turned to York, his mouth going dry at the sight that greeted him.

He was beautiful, even with the bruises and the vulnerable glint in his gaze. He finally looked straight at Leo, and Leo knew one time wouldn't be enough, and neither would two. One lifetime might be, though. He'd gone and fallen in love, and he never wanted it to end.

York was his, and he was York's, forever.

York knew he was probably being a little too rash, but he'd almost lost any chance he'd had at this. If Curt had been more brutal, or if he'd decided he didn't need York, after all, York could have been dead right now. He'd never have known what it was like to be loved by Leo and have him inside his body. He wasn't about to waste what Leo was offering.

He swallowed and leaned back, twisting his legs from under himself and straightening them as his back hit the mattress. His cheeks felt warm, and he felt he wasn't behaving like himself, but it wouldn't be enough to stop him. He rolled to his front, tucking his knees under his torso and exposing his ass in a move that would make what he wanted clear, or at least, he hoped so. He didn't think he could say the words, but he could show Leo what he yearned for.

He felt Leo move behind him and the mattress dipping as he got closer. York shivered, even though Leo hadn't touched him yet. He could imagine how Leo's hands would feel on him and how Leo would feel *inside* of him.

"You're gorgeous," Leo murmured.

He stroked a hand down York's spine. The touch was firm and his palm a little rough, no doubt from all the physical work he did in the yard. It felt so good that York wasn't sure how long he would last if Leo continued touching him that way, both reverently and like he wanted him.

York tried to turn to face Leo, knowing he'd made himself clear, but Leo gently pushed him back down. York wasn't scared, though. Leo would let him go if he asked, but he quite liked this position. He might be in love with Leo, and he wanted this desperately, but he still felt a little shy, even though he was doing his best to push that feeling away. He'd touched Leo in a way he'd never dared with anyone else, and it had made him feel powerful, but that feeling had already fizzled away. He didn't need to feel powerful, anyway. He just needed Leo.

Leo's hand moved down York's back to the curve of his ass. York's entire body flushed, and he swallowed heavily as Leo gently pulled apart his ass cheeks. York felt him move, then the sound of a drawer sliding open. He screwed his eyes shut, eager and nervous at the same time.

The sound of a cap opening was loud in the room. York stayed still, fully trusting Leo to take care of him.

Leo's hand landed on York's ass again. He'd expected it to feel slick, but it was warm and rough. He almost asked Leo what he was doing, but a rush of warm air bathed his hole and balls, making him squeak. A wet finger prodded at York's ass, and knowing that Leo was looking at that, that he was so close that York could feel his breath, made York's body feel like it was about to catch on fire. He'd never felt so open and vulnerable, yet at the same time, so loved and revered.

Leo gently massaged York before sliding a finger inside. York let out a sigh and told himself to relax. He was incredibly exposed, but he trusted Leo with his life, so why not with his body? Leo would take care of him. He'd love him and give him everything he wanted, even though he couldn't ask for it.

He'd wanted this since the first time he'd seen Leo. He'd felt horrified and guilty over what he'd done to Marcel, and he'd expected to be beaten at the very least, but he hadn't been able to stop himself from wanting Leo even then. He hadn't believed he had a chance with him then, and sometimes, he still didn't, but he couldn't deny how he felt or what was happening.

They were coming together, becoming one, all because Leo hadn't given up on York.

York pushed all thoughts away for later when Leo pushed

another finger inside him and gently pushed them apart, working York's hole so he wouldn't be hurt by what would happen next. At the same time, Leo's mouth and tongue were running up and down York's spine, leaving damp trails everywhere.

York wondered if maybe, he should do something, too, participate more instead of just lying here and letting Leo have his way with him, but this felt too good. He liked that Leo didn't have a problem taking care of him.

Leo didn't ask for more. He continued to open York up, sliding more of his blunt fingers in and moving them until York was moaning his name and trying to push back and pull away at the same time. It was too much, yet not enough. He needed more but felt he might explode if Leo gave it to him.

York arched his back, trying to get more. Leo seemed to understand him, thankfully, and after kissing a path back down to York's ass and pressing a kiss to both of his ass cheeks, he leaned back. His fingers left York's body, making him feel empty.

York knew what came next, and he couldn't wait. He raised himself into a kneeling position and turned, reaching for Leo, who welcomed him into his arms. They pressed together, their cocks meeting in the space between their bodies. York wasn't sure what to do, but thankfully, Leo took charge again. York liked that Leo knew this was what he wanted. He felt like every time he had to make a decision, he made the wrong one, and he was happy to leave control in Leo's capable hands.

Leo kissed York even as he tilted them backward. York opened his legs, making space for Leo to settle against him. Leo did so easily, like he belonged there, pressed against York's body, buried deep in his heart.

Their lips never parted as Leo moved both of them until the head of his cock pressed against York's hole. York wrapped his legs around Leo's waist even though the entire thing made him feel awkward. That feeling was easy to forget when Leo pressed down on him, pinning him down and making him feel safe, which was all he'd ever wanted.

York moaned as Leo pushed into him. York's body opened up to him, and while York wasn't sure how to feel about the fullness, his ass stretched around Leo's cock. It burned, but York wanted more.

Leo thrust slowly, giving York time to get used to him. York found himself following Leo's movements, pressing his heels into Leo's ass to hold him as close as he could as he met every one of his thrusts.

The sound of flesh against flesh filled the room, punctuated by York's moans. York was surrounded by Leo. He was around him, inside his body, and in his heart. He made York feel complete and like he was perfect the way he was, with all his flaws and his past.

York cried out when Leo's pace quickened. He was pounding into York, his cock hitting York's prostate almost every time he pushed inside, sending pleasure radiating from his groin to his entire body. It was so much, too much, especially with York's cock rubbing against Leo's hairy stomach.

York closed his eyes, his back arching as his mouth opened on a cry. Leo's rhythm faltered, his thrusts erratic as he shuddered against York. York felt Leo's cock jerk inside of him, but Leo never stopped moving. He pushed York until York couldn't take it anymore. His entire body squeezed, then released, and he cried out again as he came. A sob escaped his throat, and he buried his face against Leo's neck, holding on to him as hard as he could.

Leo rolled them until they were both on their sides again. He kissed York's eyelids, his forehead, his cheeks, and his lips, murmuring that he loved him until York stopped shuddering and his body relaxed.

It was hard for York to believe everything Leo had told him earlier, but he was starting to. The clan had come for him. Leo had taken care of him last night, making sure he ate and was comfortable. They wouldn't have done any of that if they didn't care.

Leo kissed York's forehead. "Everything okay in there?" he asked softly.

Even after everything that happened to him, York couldn't help but smile. "I'm fine." Everything ached, and the sex hadn't helped, but he didn't care. He wouldn't have changed any of this even if he could have.

Well, he wouldn't have wanted to be kidnapped, but in the end, he was all right. He also wouldn't have found Cooper if he hadn't gotten to Curt, so he couldn't even regret what had happened.

He'd never do anything that stupid again, though.

"We don't have to go downstairs if you don't feel up for it," Leo said.

York knew what was waiting for him down there. Everyone who'd wanted to talk to him and make sure he was all right yesterday would be there. Elijah would be, too, and he'd want to know what had happened with Curt. Normally, York wouldn't want to even think about it, but he'd made a promise to his brother, and the sooner he kept it, the better it would be. There was no way to know how Curt was treating Valerian, and York didn't want to risk it. He'd been with Curt long enough to know it couldn't be good, even if Curt wasn't as cruel to Valerian as he'd been with York.

"I'm fine," he repeated.

Leo's expression told him he didn't believe him. It was probably because Leo could see all the bruises in the light of day, so York didn't blame him. His entire body ached, and he wished he could stay in bed forever, but people were waiting for him even if he hadn't made any promises. They cared about him and wanted to make sure he was all right.

And he finally believed that.

He wanted to see the clan. He wanted to talk to Elijah and reassure Marcel and his parents that he was fine. He wanted to allow Tim to hug him so he could feel for himself that York was all right.

York had been part of the clan, even though he hadn't realized it. That meant taking care of the clan members just like they took care of him.

"What's happening in that head of yours?" Leo asked. "I can't read you."

"Good."

Leo blinked. "You don't want me to be able to tell how you feel?"

"I want to be a mystery to you."

Leo laughed. "Don't worry. You already are. I don't understand you most of the time, but I don't need to in order to love you."

York's heart skipped a beat. Leo had told him he loved him earlier, too, but it was still hard to believe. There was nothing more York wanted, though. "Say it again," he whispered.

Leo's smile was gentle. "I love you. I started loving you when you were hiding in your bedroom and thinking you were useless, and I love you even more now that you finally realize that's not the case."

"How do you know?"

"I'm not sure. It's something in your expression and in the way you hold yourself. You've always been extremely tense before, as if you expected the clan to kick you out at any moment. You're relaxed now. I'd like to think it's because you're in my arms, but I know it's not only that."

He was right. It wasn't just that York was in Leo's bed. It wasn't only that Leo loved him, and he loved Leo. It was also that he'd found his brother, and even more so, that he'd found a family he'd never believed he'd have.

York leaned forward and kissed Leo's cheek. "You're right, like always. I can see that the clan truly wants me now."

"Good. I'll make sure you never forget it."

"I don't think I will." How could he when he was surrounded by love and kindness?

CHAPTER TWELVE

Even after talking to Leo and finally seeing how much the clan cared, York was nervous when they left Leo's bedroom. Thankfully, Leo took his hand, silently telling him he was there and that he wasn't going anywhere. It was all York needed to relax, and by the time he and Leo reached the conference room, he was even smiling.

All these new feelings and the knowledge that he belonged didn't help heal the pain his body was in, but that would take time. As long as he wasn't in Curt's hands anymore, York was happy.

But he'd be happier if his brother were with him.

When he walked into the conference room, it was to find that everyone was already there. They all got to their feet and made a line to say hello, even Victor's brothers, who York barely knew. Everyone seemed happy to have him back, and when the little voice in the back of his mind told him it was probably all a lie or that he was misreading things, he ignored it. He was wanted, dammit.

As soon as everyone was done saying hello, Leo pushed York toward the table. Instead of sitting next to the plant like he had the last time he'd been here, York settled there, with Leo next to him. Everyone else took their place around the table, and Marcel pushed a plate full of pastries toward York.

"I know it's not our usual breakfast, but we felt like celebrating today," he explained.

York chose a pink doughnut with a smile on his face. "Thank you." He took a bite, chewed and swallowed, then looked around. Everyone was getting coffee and tea, and a few people were eating. It helped him relax even more, and once again, he reminded himself that he belonged.

When Elijah cleared his throat, everyone's attention turned back to York. It made him want to wiggle in his seat, but instead, he looked straight at the leader.

"Thank you."

"It was a pleasure," Elijah said. He was smiling like everyone around the table.

Well, everyone but Jerome, but then he only smiled at his boyfriend.

York sucked in a breath and got ready to relive what he'd gone through with Curt. "I was an idiot. I thought I could get information out of Curt and maybe convince him the clan had kept me prisoner, but he seems to know you guys well. He said you'd never do something like that, and he didn't come alone. He had two cockatrice shifters with him, and they grabbed me and dragged me into a van."

"That must have been terrifying," Victor whispered. He reached for York's hand over the table, and York gave it a quick squeeze before pulling back. He loved that Victor cared, but he needed Leo.

Thankfully, Leo seemed to understand that and took York's hand, linking their fingers together and raising both their hands to kiss the back of York's. York took courage in that gesture, enough that he could continue explaining.

"They took me into cockatrice territory. They locked me into a bedroom, and Curt came every day to try to convince me to work for him. He kept telling me that you wouldn't come for me, that I didn't matter, and I think he truly believed that. I don't matter to him, so why should I matter to you?"

"You do matter," Leo whispered.

"I know." York's eyes burned with tears, but this time, they were happy ones. He'd found his place in the world, and he hadn't even believed he had one.

He cleared his throat. "They fed me, and the guy who brought me food was nice. Curt was the only one who hurt me. That first day, after he left me alone, my brother appeared. I yelled at him because I'd been trying to contact him for forever, but he never came. He apologized and told me that in the beginning, he didn't even understand that he was dead. Then, once he did, he drifted around for a while until he found Valerian."

"That's the man you promised you'd save," Elijah said.

"I promised Cooper I'd try, yes. I don't know much about Valerian. I've never even seen him. But Cooper told me that he'd found Valerian locked in a bedroom. He's a psychic and a mage, which is why Curt wants to use him. He's more powerful than Curt's girlfriend. Valerian doesn't have anyone left that Curt can threaten, though, and he's been holding strong. I don't know if Curt has been hurting him the way he was hurting me, but if I had to bet, I'd say yes. Thankfully, Valerian wasn't completely alone. He and my brother became friends, and Cooper is worried about him. That's why he didn't come when I called him. He didn't want to leave Valerian alone."

"So Valerian is powerful enough that Curt needs him to do whatever he's planning," Elijah said slowly.

"That's the impression I got. I never talked to him, but Cooper assured me he'd welcome the clan's help, and he needs us." York hesitated. "I might have told my brother that the clan would welcome Valerian if he didn't have anywhere else to go. I realize I shouldn't have, but I finally have Cooper back. I'd do anything to keep him with me, and I'm pretty sure that if Valerian walks, Cooper will go with him."

"I can't make promises until I meet Valerian, but I'm not opposed to having him become part of the clan. A war is brewing, and we'll need all the help we can get."

"So you'll rescue him even though we could start a war with the cockatrices?" That was what York was most afraid of. He remembered when they'd talked about what to do about Curt, and everyone had agreed to stay away because he was hiding in cockatrice territory.

"I suspect that no matter what we do, the cockatrices will find a reason to attack us," Elijah told him with a smile. "I'm not ready to start it, so we'll have to plan this rescue mission carefully. I don't want to leave anyone in their clutches if we can avoid it. I won't put the clan in danger for someone I don't even know, but we'll try. We recently welcomed you and many other people, so that won't be a problem. What's one more psychic in need?"

York was relieved and hoped Valerian would help them fight Curt and the cockatrices. Even if he didn't, he didn't deserve to be left there. York's main fear was that Valerian would decide to leave and that Cooper would go with him, but even if that happened, he and Cooper had talked. Cooper knew to come when York called for him, and hopefully, he'd stop resisting once Valerian was safe.

Either way, they couldn't leave Valerian with Curt. York might have to sacrifice his relationship with his brother, but he was ready to do just that if it meant Valerian was safe and Curt got the smack-down he deserved.

"We should go as soon as possible, maybe even today," York said.

It was good to see how easily he was talking to Elijah. Leo hadn't expected that, but clearly, York had finally realized he was a clan member and that no one meant him any harm.

Elijah raised a hand. Leo's stomach churned, knowing what his leader was about to say. He should have expected it. York was focused on his brother and Valerian, so it made sense he hadn't. Leo had no excuse.

"I said we'd help Valerian, but we have to be careful," Elijah said. "We snuck into cockatrice territory and grabbed someone from under their noses once. They won't let us do it a second time."

York stared. "But you just said you'd help him."

"We will. We just need to take some time to gather more information and find out how the cockatrices react to what happened yesterday. They'll probably put out more guards, and I'd still like to avoid starting a war with them."

"We can't leave Valerian there," York protested. "They're going to hurt him. *Curt* is going to hurt him."

And the bruises visible to everyone on his face were testimony that Curt didn't mind hurting people who didn't do what he wanted.

The thought made Leo want to leave the room and find Curt, so he sucked in a breath and focused on York instead.

"I'm really sorry," Elijah said. He did sound sorry.

Leo knew him better than York, so he could tell his leader wished he could go after Valerian right now. Everyone did. They didn't want to leave Valerian in Curt's hands any more than York, but York was emotional. Elijah's first instinct was always to protect the clan, and that was what he was aiming for. York, not so much, although no one would blame him for that.

York flopped back in his chair. "I get it. You have to think of the clan first."

He sounded resigned, but Leo narrowed his eyes at him. York was timid most of the time, but he wasn't a quitter, especially when it came to people he cared about. He'd been convinced he'd eventually get Cooper to come to him, and he hadn't stopped trying. Now, he wanted to get Valerian out of cockatrice territory, and nothing would stop him from doing just that.

He was going to do something stupid.

Leo could tell. It was in how York had set his jaw and how he was staring at Elijah as if he'd betrayed him. He understood why York felt that way, but he couldn't allow him to return to cockatrice territory alone. There would be no convincing Elijah to do something sooner, though. He was right. It could be too dangerous for the clan, and they couldn't afford to make enemies out of the cockatrices sooner than necessary.

But York wouldn't stay back. He'd already snuck out alone once, and Leo wouldn't let him do it a second time.

He sighed, hoping the other people around the table hadn't noticed. He was going to have to go with York, wasn't he?

He wished he could involve the others, but he knew better. It would be dangerous, and they risked being found and imprisoned. Elijah would be pissed if that happened. He'd be pissed once he found out what they'd done, but York wasn't going to stay back, and Leo couldn't risk losing him. He'd thought he'd go nuts when Curt had taken York. He wasn't going through that again, especially if there was something he could do to stop it.

He kept his mouth shut no matter how much he wanted to call out York for what he was planning. He focused on what Elijah was saying and continued staring at York. Did he really think no one had noticed that he was planning something? At the very least, he should have expected Leo to do so, but Leo was pretty sure he wasn't the only one. He could see Tim staring at York, and when their gazes crossed, Leo knew Tim had seen what he had.

He cleared his throat, interrupting the conversation Elijah was having with Jerome. Everyone stared, but Leo didn't care. "We need to rethink helping Valerian right away," he declared.

Elijah frowned. "We've already been through this. We

can't afford to go right now."

"I know why you believe that, and you might not be wrong, but we can't leave him there more than necessary. He's been taken and is probably being beaten every day. You wouldn't leave a clan member there, no matter what saving them meant or resulted in. The fact that Valerian isn't one of us yet shouldn't change that. He needs our help sooner rather than later."

"I agree, but I don't see what we can do without more information. I'm not sending people in blind."

"The same thing we did for York. Send a small team to rescue Valerian. We can sneak in and out easily like we did once already."

"But the cockatrices will expect you."

"Maybe not. They're unaware that York knows Valerian is there. He wouldn't have found out if it weren't for his brother, and Curt isn't a psychic. He has no way of knowing about Cooper, so he wouldn't know that Cooper and York had found each other again and that Cooper told York about Valerian."

"That doesn't mean the cockatrices won't be more careful than before."

"Which is exactly why we should go sooner rather than later. That way, they won't have the time to put up more guards or even move Valerian. Besides, we have someone inside that no one is aware of. As long as one of the psychics comes with us, we'll be able to talk to Cooper. We can also send Kenneth in, see what he finds out. They'll be able to tell us about the guards and any additional security. If the cockatrices move Valerian, it might be impossible for us to find him again."

A small hand grabbed Leo's under the table. Leo didn't have to look to know it belonged to York. York clung to Leo's hand, silently telling him he was on his side.

Just like Leo was on his, which was the only reason Leo was doing this. He disliked going against his leader, especially when Elijah had never steered them wrong, but he could see where York was coming from. Worse, he could see that York would do something stupid if he didn't step in, and he didn't think his heart could stand going through that a second time.

Elijah sighed. "We're going to need at least today and tomorrow to go over this. We all want to help Valerian, but it won't do us any good if we get captured or worse. At the end of tomorrow, we'll go over what we know and what the ghosts have been able to tell us, and I'll make a decision."

Elijah's tone was uncompromising, and Leo knew him well enough to be aware of the fact that nothing he could do or say would push Elijah to change his mind. York probably realized it, too, which meant he'd move on his own even though he'd promised he wouldn't.

Leo looked at him. York was biting his lower lip, clearly lost in his thoughts. What was he going to do? Sneak out while everyone was sleeping? It was what Leo would do, which meant he'd have to keep an eye on York.

York noticed him staring and smiled, but it wasn't natural. "I promise I won't do anything stupid," he said.

"We might have a different opinion of what stupid means."

York shook his head. "After everything the clan has done for me, I can't put myself in danger again."

York was saying all the right things, but Leo still didn't trust him. He didn't blame him. He wanted to save Valerian, too. He understood why York was so frantic about it.

York would never ask Leo to disobey Elijah and go with him, but he didn't have to. Leo's loyalty had always been to the clan and Elijah, but that had changed since York had barged into his life. Now, *he* was the most important person in Leo's life. Leo couldn't abandon him, but it was clear York wasn't about to tell him what he was plotting.

Which meant Leo would have to find out on his own.

CHAPTER THIRTEEN

This day had been one of the longest in Leo's life. It had started with him and York in bed, confessing their feelings to each other. It had continued with the meeting in which York had told everyone what happened to him, and it had ended with York in Leo's bed again.

Leo was pretty sure York wasn't asleep. He was acting like he was, snuggling his pillow and breathing evenly, but York was planning something, no doubt something stupid. Leo wasn't sure what it said of him that he was ready to go along with it, but he supposed it didn't matter.

Besides, he agreed with York that they needed to rescue Valerian as soon as possible, mostly because he wouldn't be surprised if Curt moved him. It wasn't just that they needed to keep Valerian away from him because no one deserved to be treated the way Curt was no doubt treating him. It was also that Valerian could be an important weapon for Curt, and the clan should get their hands on him before Valerian broke and gave Curt what he wanted.

More importantly, York wouldn't be going anywhere on his own. Leo had almost lost him once and wasn't willing to go through that again. Where York went, he went, too.

So Leo did a little acting of his own. He regulated his breathing, almost smiling when he felt York move next to him. His movements were slow, and Leo was pretty sure that he leaned closer to check if he was sleeping. Leo kept his eyes shut and his breathing regular, and after a moment, he felt York slide away and get out of bed.

They were going to have a conversation about sneaking out and doing stupid things, but not now.

Leo wanted nothing more than to go after York right away, but he waited. Leo shot out of bed as soon as the bedroom door closed behind York. He'd been expecting this, so he'd gotten his clothes ready. It only took him a few moments to grab them and put them on, along with his boots. Then he carefully opened the bedroom door and peeked out.

York was nowhere to be seen.

Leo hurried down the hallway, knowing where York was headed. He'd need a mode of transportation to cockatrice territory, and the easiest one would be Leo's car. Leo had made sure to leave the keys out because he didn't want York to freak out, and besides, he'd planned on them going together. If York thought he was doing this on his own, he was sorely mistaken.

Leo had to hurry, because York had been faster than he'd expected. By the time he reached the front door, he could hear the car had been started. He rushed out the door, managing to place himself into the car's path just in time. York slammed on the brakes, for which Leo was grateful, and they stared at each other.

Even though the night was dark, Leo could see York's wide eyes and his horrified expression. He put his hands on his hips and arched a brow, waiting for whatever York was about to say.

"It's not what you think," York said as he opened the door and got out.

"Isn't it? Because I think this is you sneaking out of the house to go rescue Valerian on your own and doing something stupid, even though you promised you wouldn't."

York shuffled his feet. He hadn't turned the car off, and the lights were still on, illuminating him from behind. "Okay, then maybe it *is* what you think. I'm sorry."

Leo sucked in a breath. "I sure hope you are. You made a promise, and you broke it."

York raised his chin. "I'd break it again if it meant rescuing Valerian. Even though I told you, you don't know what it was like. I can't leave him there."

"I don't disagree. You shouldn't have snuck out on your own, though. I thought we'd agreed we were in this together."

"We are, but I can't ask you to come with me and put yourself in danger, along with disobeying Elijah's orders. I can't risk you getting kicked out of the clan."

Leo hadn't considered that possibility, but he doubted it would happen. Elijah would be pissed, but he could deal with that if it meant keeping York safe.

"He's not going to kick us out of the clan," he said, striding toward York.

York stood his ground, which was good to see. Leo didn't want him to be afraid.

He leaned closer and cupped York's cheek. "You're not alone anymore," he murmured. "You should remember that. The clan and Elijah are important to me, but you're more important. You always will be."

"I can't ask you to betray Elijah and the clan."

"Then it's a good thing you're not asking me to do that. I agree with you *and* Elijah. We need to rescue Valerian, and we should be careful about it. I understand why Elijah wants to take his time, but I also see where you're coming from. We don't *have* time."

"Curt is going to do something. I know it."

"And I believe you. Which is why I'm going with you, and together, we'll rescue Valerian."

"You're sure Elijah won't kick you out?"

"Positive. And even if he does, it doesn't matter."

York shook his head. "How can you say that?"

"I'm doing the right thing. Valerian is clearly important to you, which means he's important to me."

"I've never even met him."

"Does it matter? He means something to Cooper, and Cooper's your brother. If you're going, I am, too."

York's shoulders slumped. "I won't be able to change your mind, will I?"

"No. I guess you'll be the one to make the big decision and decide if we're both staying home or if we're both going." And Leo already knew York wasn't staying.

York nodded. "We're going."

Leo wasn't one bit surprised. "I'll drive," he said, sliding into the driver's seat.

York settled next to him in the passenger seat. He didn't say anything as Leo pulled away, but Leo didn't expect that to last long. He knew he was right when, after a few minutes, York twisted in his seat to look at him.

"Why are you doing this?"

"Mainly, I'm doing it for you. You're throwing yourself into danger again, and I can't allow that to happen. You'll rescue Valerian no matter what I say or do, so I might as well help you."

"You said that mainly you're doing it for me."

"I understand what you're going through, at least in part. When I thought I'd lost Marcel, I was angry and ready to do pretty much anything to get him back. I'd have done something stupid like going to rescue him in cockatrice territory if I'd needed to, even against Elijah's orders."

"Which is what we're about to do."

"Exactly. Love makes you do stupid things, and I can't blame you for any of this. No one will, even after they find out about our little trip." Or at least, Leo hoped that would be the case.

He already knew most people would be pissed. Tim and

Marcel would understand, though. They'd probably be miffed that Leo and York hadn't brought them along, especially Tim.

But this was something they needed to do on their own. They couldn't risk Elijah or anyone else trying to stop them, but as he drove away, Leo wished they'd told someone. He and York were risking a lot by going alone.

He hoped it would be worth it.

York should have known this wouldn't be as easy as he'd hoped. He'd thought the hard part would come once he got to cockatrice territory, but he should have known Leo had realized he was planning something and had decided to stick his nose into it.

York was happy to have Leo with him. He'd been terrified of going to cockatrice territory on his own, so he couldn't deny that having Leo with him helped. The last thing he'd wanted was to put Leo in danger, though, and that was precisely what he was doing. He hadn't been sure he'd come back, and he'd been ready to sacrifice himself if it meant helping Valerian, but now he'd also be sacrificing Leo, and that wasn't something he could deal with.

But he was going to have to.

There was no convincing Leo to stay back. York had tried, although not very hard. He didn't *want* Leo to go back.

Actually, if he had his way, they'd both turn around and go home, convince Elijah he needed to help, and go with the rest of the group. Elijah had already said they wouldn't be going anywhere until at least tomorrow night, though, and that felt like too long for Valerian. Elijah didn't fully understand what spending that time with Curt was like. He hadn't been in Valerian's place, but York had, and he wouldn't let even his worst enemy go through something like that.

Except maybe Curt.

Curt deserved everything bad the universe wanted to give him. The problem was that, like most evil people, he never got what he deserved.

"You're nervous," Leo said. He didn't look at York, but he didn't need to.

York was bouncing his knee, and yes, he was nervous. "Aren't you?"

"I guess I am. I've already been in this position, though. I know what I'm about to face. It would be easier if we had the others with us, but we can do this."

York wasn't sure they could, but he couldn't focus on that or on what would happen. He was afraid that something bad would happen to Leo, and he wouldn't be able to live with himself if that was the case. It would be his fault. That was why he'd decided to do this on his own, but he should have known better.

Leo drove them toward whatever Curt was planning for them while York tried to breathe. York hoped Curt hadn't realized they knew about Valerian, but he wouldn't put anything past the asshole. Thankfully, Curt wasn't a psychic, and York hadn't seen his girlfriend anywhere in the house when he'd been there, so hopefully, they'd be safe.

It was still hard to breathe.

But York understood why Leo was here. If their roles had been reversed, he wouldn't have let Leo do this on his own, either. He didn't like the thought of putting the man he loved in danger, but Leo was the one who needed to make that decision, just like York had decided not to wait for the clan to help. He knew what he was doing, or at least, he hoped so. He had to have the same trust in Leo.

"What will we do when we get there?" he asked in a whisper.

"You haven't thought about it?"

"I should have, but honestly, the only thing I thought of was that I needed to get to Cooper."

Leo nodded as if he wasn't surprised. "Well, I know the way to the house. We'll be as quiet as possible as we head there."

"I'd probably have been captured if I'd gone on my own."

Leo didn't look amused. "I have no doubt you would have been. I hate that you felt you had to do this alone."

"You heard Elijah."

"I did, but I'm not Elijah. You should have at least told me."

"I didn't want to put you against the clan. They're your family."

"And you're the man I love. That takes precedence."

It was still hard for York to wrap his mind around that, but he should stop trying to convince himself he didn't matter as much as the clan. Leo had made his decision, and he'd picked a side.

He'd chosen York.

Leo didn't say anything about the fact that York was still bouncing his knee. York became more and more nervous as they got closer to cockatrice territory, and by the time Leo parked the car in the middle of a small bunch of trees and bushes, he felt ready to jump out of his skin. The darkness around them was deep, which would no doubt be a good thing when they reached the house, but for now, it only made York more nervous.

He could hear the engine of the car ticking as it cooled down. He was afraid to look at Leo, but they couldn't stay here much longer.

"Do you think you could call Cooper?" Leo asked.

York was an idiot because he hadn't even thought about it. "He promised he'd come from now on."

"Good. Try it."

York could do that from inside the car, but he decided it

would be awkward, so he opened the door and slid out. He closed it as gently as possible so he wouldn't make too much noise, then he stood there, his heart racing. He closed his eyes, knowing Leo would have his back. If someone found them and attacked, Leo wouldn't allow anything to happen to York.

Instead of focusing on Leo, York turned his thoughts to his brother. He imagined Cooper as he'd been when they were kids, and as soon as he had a good image in his mind, he pulled.

It was an odd feeling, but this time, there was a lot less resistance than he was used to when he did this. That alone was enough to tell him that Cooper had been resisting every time he'd tried pulling him close in the past. He'd wanted to stay with Valerian, so it made sense, but York still wished his brother hadn't done that. He wished he'd known what was happening to Cooper and Valerian. Maybe if he had, they'd have been able to rescue Valerian a while ago.

"York?"

Cooper's voice startled York, and he opened his eyes to find his brother standing in front of him. He beamed, even though there was little to smile about in this situation. "You came."

"I told you I would. What's going on?"

"We're here to rescue Valerian."

Cooper's eyes widened. "Already?" He looked around. "Where is everyone?"

York didn't want to lie to his brother, but he also didn't want Cooper to freak out. "It's just Leo and me."

Cooper narrowed his eyes. "What do you mean?"

"We thought it would be better if it were only a few of us. That way, there are fewer chances we'll be found out."

"You're acting on your own, aren't you? You talked about the clan so much, but they didn't want to do this."

York sighed. "They did, but Elijah, the clan leader, wanted more information and time. The clan decided to come tomorrow evening."

"Yet you're here tonight."

"Because they don't know Curt the way I do. They don't know what he can do, and what I have no doubt he's doing to Valerian. Having gone through the same thing, I couldn't leave him here any longer than necessary. That's why I decided to come."

Cooper didn't look convinced. "What if the cockatrices hear you?"

"It's only the two of us. I know you don't have much trust in me, but I promise we'll do everything we can."

Cooper frowned. "I never said I didn't trust you. I just need Valerian to be okay."

"And he will be. Once we're out of here, we'll take him straight to the clan. We'll take both of you."

Cooper stared for a moment before nodding. "All right. I trust you."

That meant a lot to York. He'd never wanted to hug his brother more than he did now, but unfortunately, he couldn't. So, instead, he turned to Leo. "Cooper will help us."

"Good. He needs to tell us if there are any more guards this time around."

"There aren't," Cooper told York. "Curt wanted more of them, but the cockatrice alpha refused. He said that since no one knows about Valerian, there was no need. I think it's because he doesn't have many people. He's also not as involved as Curt, so he doesn't see losing you or Valerian like a bad thing. Quite the contrary, actually. You were two mouths to feed that he didn't want anything to do with. The only reason he'd agreed to keep you here was that Curt promised he'd be the one to take care of you."

York repeated the message, relieved when Leo took charge.

"Let's go," Leo said as he started walking in the direction of the house where York had been kept prisoner.

York was terrified, but he'd follow Leo anywhere, even deep into cockatrice territory.

Following the directions of someone he couldn't see made Leo nervous, but York trusted his brother, and Leo trusted York. He doubted Cooper was setting up a trap for them. Whoever Valerian was, he was important to Cooper, enough that Cooper had stayed with him and away from his only brother to make sure he was all right.

All of that would end tonight.

Leo was doing this for York, but he couldn't deny he was curious about Valerian. Knowing that he was both a psychic and a mage meant Leo understood why Curt wanted him, but what could Valerian actually do? Leo wouldn't find out until he met Valerian, and that wouldn't happen until he and York snuck into the house.

Which he was more than ready to do.

Apparently, York had sent his brother ahead, and every so often, Cooper came back and told York about the situation waiting for them. It meant they knew there were no guards to avoid until they reached the house. There was one there, but York explained it was Terrence, the one who'd been feeding him. That didn't mean Leo trusted the guy, but he didn't need to trust him to kick his ass.

He swallowed once they reached the house. Last time, he hadn't needed to go inside. He would this time, and he didn't feel right about having York with him. Unfortunately, he couldn't leave York outside because he was the only one of them who could talk to Cooper. Leo supposed he should be relieved they had at least that. Sending the ghost ahead meant they'd be able to avoid getting caught, or at least, Leo hoped so.

They paused by the back door, and York turned to look at Leo. "Cooper's gone inside. He said he was going upstairs to tell Valerian we're here, then he'd do a quick round of the house to find Terrence."

"Good."

"I'm really sorry about all of this."

Leo shook his head. "Don't be. We're doing the right thing." He was convinced of that, even though he wished they had more help. Even having Jerome at his back would have made him feel better.

Thankfully, they didn't have to wait long for Cooper to come back. York smiled, and Leo knew it was because his brother was there.

"He says everything is clear," York said.

"Lead the way," Leo told him, stepping aside.

It didn't sit right with him or his dragon to let York walk in first, so he stayed as close as he could without being a hindrance. He followed York through the kitchen and out of it, stepping into the hallway. They had to follow it to reach the stairs, but no one tried to stop them. Leo really hoped that this Terrence guy was the only cockatrice shifter here. He could always shift and attack, but it would be better if the cockatrices didn't know they were here. If what Cooper had said was right and the cockatrices didn't care about Valerian, they wouldn't have a problem with him going missing. Curt would, but that was what they were aiming for. Leo wanted Curt to be frustrated and angry. Maybe the guy would make a mistake, which they sorely needed him to do, especially now that he had the protection of the cockatrice shifters.

Leo gritted his teeth as they climbed the creaking stairs. He couldn't hear anyone, but Cooper had said Terrence was around. Where? Was he downstairs or upstairs? Leo should have asked before, but he didn't want Terrence to hear him, so it was too late. He'd have to deal with not knowing where the cockatrice was. Hopefully, they wouldn't even see him from afar.

Once they got upstairs, they turned left, following the hallway. Leo wondered where York had been kept, but he didn't dare ask. He didn't want to remind York of what had happened to him only days before.

Eventually, they reached a closed door. York turned, nodding at Leo, and since Leo knew York had unlocked the door of the room he'd been kept in, he let York do his thing. It was better that way, anyway. He could keep an eye on York while also making sure no one snuck up behind them.

The sound of the lock opening made Leo jump. It felt too loud in the silent house, and both he and York froze, expecting Terrence to come running. Nothing happened, though, and after looking at Leo one last time, York straightened his back and pushed open the door.

Leo wasn't sure what he'd been expecting from Valerian. He didn't even have a description of the man, but he wasn't surprised to see that, like York, Valerian's skin was marred with bruises. He was huddled on the bed, his back plastered against the wall, staring at Leo and York.

Valerian's dark hair hung in front of his frightened eyes. They were the color of a storm, a deep gray that Leo suspected was made darker by fear. He didn't know what to do, but he stayed by the door as York stepped closer. He was at a disadvantage because he was the only one who couldn't hear or see Cooper. Both York and Valerian were staring at the empty space by the foot of the bed, and Leo knew that was where Cooper had to be. Whatever he was saying, it was enough for Valerian to get up, even though his legs shook. When he did so, Leo saw how thin he was. Was Curt even feeding him? If he needed Valerian, shouldn't he be keeping him in a good state?

"You're here to get me out?" Valerian asked.

York nodded and stepped even closer. "Cooper helped me escape last night, and I couldn't let you stay here one more night. I know what you're going through. I've been there, too."

Valerian and York were more or less the same height, so when Valerian leaned against York, it didn't take much for York to wrap an arm around his shoulders and hold him up. Leo hurried to their side, needing to be useful. Valerian jerked back, but York was quick to soothe him.

"This is my boyfriend, Leo. He can't see Cooper because he's not a psychic, but he'll help us get out. You can trust him."

It was humbling to hear those words coming from York, especially considering everything he'd gone through.

Leo was relieved when Valerian allowed him to take more of his weight. He was probably their best fighting chance if someone found them, but it didn't sit right with him to let York help Valerian on his own, even though Valerian was strong enough to walk.

Valerian didn't seem convinced, but one look at the empty space next to him, and he nodded. Leo might never be able to see or talk to Cooper, but he was grateful the man was on their side. He suspected Cooper was the only reason Valerian trusted him and York to get him out.

Once again, York sent Cooper ahead so he could make sure the hallway was empty. Leo realized it would be stupid for him to stay back with Valerian when York was doing a good job helping him. He placed himself in front of them instead, even though he wouldn't know if someone was coming. Hopefully, they'd have enough warning between Cooper and York.

They made their way downstairs more slowly than they'd gone upstairs, and every additional second made Leo's

A Psychic in Need

stomach churn. The house sounded empty, but York had said that Cooper had mentioned at least one cockatrice shifter was around. Where was he? Wasn't he supposed to be a guard? How could he do that if he wasn't in the house? And if he was in the house, why couldn't Leo hear him? How had Terrence not noticed he and Valerian weren't alone anymore?

Leo didn't like anything about this, but he didn't know what else to do. The only way he could help was by getting Valerian and York out—ASAP.

Cooper was hovering close, even though York had told him to go ahead and keep an eye on Terrence if he could. York wasn't sure Terrence would raise the alarm if he found them, but he couldn't risk it, especially after what had happened the night before. He didn't know what exactly Curt had done to Terrence for letting York escape under his nose, but it couldn't have been good.

Valerian was having a hard time lifting his feet, so they were shuffling ahead more than walking, which slowed them down. There was nothing York could do about it. He wasn't strong enough to carry Valerian, even though the man was frightfully thin, even more than York had been when he'd been rescued along with Marcel.

"Cooper," York said through gritted teeth. He didn't want Leo to realize Cooper wasn't doing his job. "Where's Terrence?"

Cooper glared. "Not here."

"You can't know that because you're not looking for him. Go. Leo and I will get Valerian to the back door, but what do you think will happen if Terrence finds us? We need you to make sure he's not around."

Cooper glared but disappeared as they started walking down the stairs. Valerian had to cling to the banister, but they

165

managed, even though he was panting by the time they reached the last step.

"Didn't they feed you?" Leo grumbled.

"I ate as little as possible," Valerian explained in a soft voice York could barely hear. "I was afraid they'd do something to the food, even after Terrence reassured me it was fine. I started eating more recently, but it clearly hasn't been enough."

That was an understatement, but York had done the same thing, so he wasn't about to blame Valerian.

"Almost there," Leo whispered as they got to the end of the hallway that led from the stairs to the kitchen.

That was when everything went to shit.

Cooper appeared in front of York, his eyes wide as saucers. Even without asking, York knew what had happened, and he opened his mouth to tell Leo that Terrence was in the kitchen. Leo had already stepped in, though, and while he retreated backward toward York, Terrence had already seen him.

Terrence had been at the sink, drying his hands. He was still holding the towel, its white color a harsh contrast with the bruises on Terrence's face and arms. Curt had clearly gotten to him, and while Terrence was technically working with Curt, York suspected it wasn't because he wanted to. His family had been threatened, and that would be enough for most people to go along with Curt, no matter how horrifying what he asked was.

Leo started moving forward, possibly to attack Terrence, but Terrence raised both hands and quickly went back, pressing against the kitchen counter. "I won't stop you," he said.

Leo stopped moving, but he stayed between Terrence and Valerian and York. Cooper hovered there, clearly wanting to intervene, but neither Terrence nor Leo could see him.

York would never forgive himself if someone got hurt, even Terrence. He couldn't forget that Terrence had been nice to him, even though he hadn't let him go.

But what now? They could all stay here, staring at each other. Terrence had said he wouldn't stop them, and maybe he really wouldn't, but how were they supposed to trust him? And even if they did, how were they supposed to leave and abandon Terrence to a fate that York intimately knew would be painful?

CHAPTER FOURTEEN

The cockatrice shifter had to be Terrence. It was the only explanation that made sense, because he hadn't attacked yet. If he did, Leo would defend himself, Valerian, and York. He didn't care who he had to kill in order to make it out of this place alive and with the man he loved.

Terrence was still staring at them. He was in bad shape, like Valerian and York, which made Leo feel sorry for him. He wasn't sure he could afford to feel that way, though, and he took a step forward, needing to get York and Valerian out of this place.

"Don't hurt him," Valerian quickly said.

Leo froze. "He's a cockatrice shifter. He kept you prisoner," he said slowly without looking back.

The hand on his arm surprised him. Valerian slowly walked past him, coming to stand between him and Terrence. "He is, but he tried helping me. He's not the one who hurt me. He's not a bad person."

Leo wasn't sure about that, but he could see that Terrence was a victim as much as York and Valerian. He'd probably been beaten because York had escaped, and it was easy to imagine what would happen to him once Curt realized Valerian was gone, too.

Leo nodded, hoping he wouldn't regret it. That seemed to spur Terrence into action. He looked from them to the hallway from which they'd come, his eyes wide. "What are you doing?"

"We're leaving," Leo snapped at him. He tried to gentle his

voice because both Valerian and York seemed to trust the poor guy. "York and I came to rescue Valerian."

"Curt is coming," Terrence said quickly, moving to peer out in the hallway. "You have to go."

"Come with us," Valerian begged.

Leo almost groaned. He understood wanting to help Terrence and even agreed with it, but was it a good idea?

Terrence was already shaking his head. "I can't."

"You know what's going to happen if you don't come," Valerian said, stepping closer. He raised a hand and gently touched Terrence his cheek. "What he's doing to you is unfair."

"I never said it was fair. I can't go, though."

Valerian looked like he wanted to protest, but they didn't have time for this. "Do you know where the clan is?" Leo asked.

Terrence stared at him. "The dragon clan?"

"Yes."

"Everyone knows where the dragon clan is."

"Good. If you ever manage to find a way out of this situation, come to us. I'll vouch for you."

"Why would you do that?"

"Because you could have made the situation worse for York, but you didn't. He told me you tried helping, even though it didn't do much. He also said you probably would have let him go if your family hadn't been involved."

Terrence grimaced. "He's right. I'm sorry I couldn't do more."

"You did plenty," York reassured him.

Leo wasn't sure about that, but who was he to protest any of this? He hadn't been a prisoner like Valerian and York. Valerian especially seemed to trust Terrence, and he'd been here a while.

"You have to leave," Terrence whispered urgently. "Take

the back door. Curt always parks in the front."

"He'll hurt you," Valerian insisted.

"I know, but there's nothing I can do. I can't leave without my family."

Valerian clearly didn't want to go, but they also couldn't stay. Leo had half a mind to grab him and carry him over his shoulder, but he didn't want to do that to a guy who'd recently been beaten. The last thing he needed was to freak out Valerian.

Terrence ushered them to the back door. "There are only a few guards around," he murmured. "Our alpha didn't think they were necessary. You shouldn't have a problem leaving, just like you didn't have one coming in."

"Please," Valerian begged.

York seemed to be looking from Valerian and Terrence to an empty spot, which was probably where his brother was standing. Leo wanted to ask him what was going on, but he felt that now wasn't the right moment. The problem was that he wasn't sure there *would* be a right moment, especially if they didn't hurry.

Terrence clearly felt the same because he gently pushed Valerian toward the door. "You heard this guy. If I ever manage to get away, I'll come to the clan."

"We'll stay there," Valerian promised. "York said we could."

Leo wasn't surprised York had promised something like that. He'd asked Elijah if it was a possibility during the meeting, so he'd probably told Cooper the clan would welcome Valerian. Leo had a hard time remembering what had been said when his mind was crowded with worry and fear, but Elijah had confirmed Valerian would be welcome.

They couldn't afford for Curt to hear them and find out what they were doing. They had to get out, but it looked like Leo was going to have to drag Valerian away. He took a step forward to do just that, but York quickly shook his head and grabbed his arm.

"Cooper is talking to him," he murmured.

"I hate that I can't see him."

"I wish you could. Something's up, and I don't think it has anything to do with Curt."

Something was definitely up, because Terrence took Valerian's hand away from his cheek, kissed its palm, then lowered it. "Go," he repeated.

Valerian's shoulders shook, but he stepped away from Terrence. Terrence swallowed heavily, looking like he wanted to reach for him again. Instead, he opened the back door.

"Curt will be here soon, and he might have people with him. You can't wait until they get here to escape."

Leo took York's hand and pulled him toward the door. It was clear Valerian had feelings for Terrence, so he understood why he was so reluctant to leave. He was tempted to drag Terrence away, too, but he respected the fact that the man wasn't going anywhere unless his family was safe. He'd feel the same way if he was in his place. He just hoped Terrence wouldn't get himself killed, because that wouldn't benefit anyone.

Valerian still resisted leaving, so Leo let go of York and wrapped an arm around Valerian's shoulders. Valerian was startled and jerked away, but Leo tightened his hold. "I'm sorry about this, but we need to go. If we stay, Curt might find you, and then, you'll end up back in that room, along with York. I'll probably be killed, along with Terrence. Is that what you want?"

Valerian's eyes were full of tears. "We can't abandon him."

"I don't want to, but we also can't force him to come. The only thing he wants is for you to go. Give him at least that."

Valerian clearly wasn't happy about it, but he allowed Leo to pull him along. York had already stepped out of the house, and he looked relieved when he saw them. He took Valerian's hand, gently talking to him as they left the house behind.

Valerian kept stumbling because he was looking back, and when Leo did the same, it was to see that Terrence was staring at them from the back door. He raised a hand, and Valerian raised his.

Then, Terrence closed the door.

The light from the kitchen disappeared, leaving them in darkness. Valerian sobbed, but York was there, comforting him as well as he could without making too much noise. Leo swallowed, knowing Terrence might die in the next hour or so. It made him want to go back, but like he'd told Valerian, he couldn't drag Terrence away if Terrence was unwilling to come.

"Let's go," he said.

He and York looked at each other for a moment before York nodded. "I'll keep an eye on Valerian. You make sure no one attacks us."

Leo nodded back, more than happy to go along with York's plan. He liked that York didn't hesitate to tell him what to do. Just a few weeks ago, hell, a few *days* ago, he wouldn't have dared, but now, he seemed to understand that Leo was on his side.

And that was never going to change.

York could see that Valerian was heartbroken, which made him wonder what had happened. He'd thought for sure that Cooper and Valerian were in love, but maybe he was wrong. From the way Cooper hovered close, maybe Cooper did have feelings for Valerian, but Valerian clearly had feelings for Terrence.

Where did that leave everyone?

It was none of York's business, and now wasn't the right

moment to ask Cooper what had been happening. He focused on Valerian, knowing Cooper would follow.

They rushed between the trees, making sure to avoid guards and being as silent as possible while also being fast. Valerian was struggling, probably because he was weak from not eating much, and York was having a hard time keeping him up while also running and ensuring they didn't lose Leo.

Valerian cried out as he stumbled on a root. York had been holding onto his arm, but he went down hard, and York had to let go if he didn't want to be pulled along. He was already moving forward to help Valerian back to his feet, but he wasn't the only one. Cooper did the same, taking Valerian's arm and hauling him back up.

York's eyes went wide. How was that possible? Some ghosts were strong enough to touch objects, even to move them, but this? It shouldn't have been possible. It hadn't been when he'd tried touching Cooper and Cooper had tried touching him. Yet, Cooper hadn't hesitated to grab Valerian, and even now, he linked their hands together and pulled him along.

York stared at them. He didn't realize he was slowing down until Leo had to come back to take his hand and drag him forward, and once that happened, York shook himself. He'd have time for questions later. The most important thing now was to get everyone out of the forest and into the car, then the car out of cockatrice territory.

He moved ahead to Valerian's side, eyeing the way Valerian and Cooper were still holding hands. Instead of asking like he was dying to, he wrapped an arm around Valerian's waist and helped him walk along.

He'd never been so relieved when they finally reached the car. They hadn't heard anyone behind them, but he had no doubt that as soon as Curt realized Valerian was gone, he'd send someone after him—if he didn't come himself.

That was a terrifying thought. York never wanted to see Curt again, but unfortunately, he would have to, if anything, on the day they finally defeated him.

That day couldn't come soon enough.

Leo rushed toward the driver's door, leaving York behind to help Valerian into the car. York didn't have a problem with that because it meant that as soon as Valerian was sitting in the backseat, he rushed to the front passenger seat and slid in. The engine was already running, so it took Leo only a few seconds to get them on the road. York held his breath as they started driving, knowing he wouldn't fully relax until they were back home with the clan.

"Is everyone all right?" Leo asked after a tense moment of silence.

"I'm fine," York said, reaching over to squeeze his hand on the steering wheel.

"You really love him, don't you?" Cooper asked.

He'd sat in the backseat with Valerian, and when York twisted around to look at them, he couldn't help but notice they were still holding hands. "I do," he told his brother. "What about the two of you? Or should I say the three of you?"

Valerian's cheeks flushed, but Cooper raised his chin, his expression defiant. "What do you want to know?"

York had so many questions, and not just about Valerian and Terrence. He wanted to ask all of them, but was now the right moment? "How can the two of you touch like that?" he asked instead of asking Cooper and Valerian about their love life.

Valerian blinked. "What?"

York pointed at Valerian's hand, which was linked with Cooper's. "I've never seen anything like that. I know that some ghosts are powerful enough to pick up objects and move them, and I've seen it several times, but this is different."

Valerian nodded. "It's because of me."

"Because you're a mage and a psychic."

"Cooper told you?"

York wasn't sure what he should and shouldn't tell Valerian. He should probably be honest, though. He didn't want Valerian to be afraid of him or to hate him because of what he'd done in the past. "He did," he confirmed. "I used to work for Curt. Well, I guess he used to threaten me so I'd do his bidding. In the beginning, I did it voluntarily because he told me he'd help me get my brother back. I met his girlfriend, Melanie. I knew she was a mage and a psychic, but I wasn't sure what it meant exactly."

"Cooper told me what you've gone through. I'm sorry Curt hurt you."

"Just like I'm sorry he hurt you. All of that is in the past now, though."

Valerian looked torn. "Not for me. Not for Cooper. Terrence is still back there."

And didn't York have questions about that. It felt like a better idea to focus on what Valerian could and couldn't do. "So the fact that my brother can touch you is because you're a mage and a psychic?"

"It is. My mage magic gives him a solid form. It also makes him visible to people who aren't psychics."

York made a surprised sound and turned to peer at Leo. Leo was focused on the road, but he briefly peaked in the rearview mirror, smiling at whatever he saw there.

"It's a pleasure to meet you, Cooper," he said.

York felt faint. How was any of this possible? He'd never known that ghosts could become as solid as Cooper was now or visible to non-psychics. What Valerian could do was incredible, and York had even more questions.

"Same," Cooper said, smiling at Leo. "And you better treat

my brother right."

Leo chuckled. "I will if he allows me to. He needs to stop sneaking out of the house."

Cooper laughed, and York told himself to relax. They'd have time, or at least, he hoped so. He didn't want to lose Cooper, and clearly, Cooper and Valerian were an item. That meant that where one went, the other followed. If Valerian refused to stay with the clan, Cooper would, too, and York didn't want that to happen.

"How did you end up here?" Leo asked, briefly looking at Valerian.

Valerian sighed heavily. His eyes were drifting shut, and York wondered if that was why Leo was asking him questions. Maybe he thought it would be good for Valerian to stay awake until Albert could see him. Valerian needed a doctor, and soon.

"I'm not sure how he found out about me," Valerian explained. "I'd never advertised what I can do, although I also wasn't discreet about it. I could help people, and I was never shy about that. Curt took me one evening, and he's been keeping me in that bedroom since then. He visited often, threatening me and beating me up so I'll do what he wants. He didn't tell me what that was, and I didn't ask. It didn't matter to me because I was never going to help him." He hesitated. "I also never thought anyone would come for me. I don't have any family, and I'm pretty sure that even the people who realized I was gone didn't care much. If it hadn't been for Cooper, no one would have cared what happened to me."

"Well, you have the clan now," York said. "They can be a bit much, but they're lovely people, and they'll welcome you."

"It sounds too good to be true."

"I felt that way for a long time, but I'm starting to believe it's just how they are. I mean, I kidnapped one of their clan members and kept him in a coma. It would have been their right to kick my ass, but they never did."

"I wasn't sure what to believe when Cooper told me about you and that you'd promised the clan would help us, but now, I hope you're right. I want Cooper to have you back."

York licked his lips. "If Leo can see him, and you can touch him, does it mean I can touch him, too?" Maybe it didn't work that way. Maybe the only one who could actually touch Cooper was Valerian.

But Valerian smiled. "You can touch him as long as he and I keep touching. My power is what's making him solid."

York turned even further and reached a hand back. Cooper didn't let go of Valerian, but he had a second hand, and he held it out to York. York held his breath as their fingers brushed against each other.

He'd been looking for his brother for so long, but he'd never thought of what would happen once he found him. Now, even though Cooper was dead, York was able to grab his hand and squeeze it, something he hadn't thought he'd ever be able to do again. He owed it to Valerian, and right there and then, York promised himself that whatever Valerian needed, York would make sure he had it.

CHAPTER FIFTEEN

L eo had hoped that everyone would still be asleep when they got home. It was the middle of the night, so it would have made sense for everyone to be in their beds.

He should have known better.

All the lights downstairs were on as he parked the car in front of the house. He and York looked at each other, and York finally let go of his brother's hand. He settled back in his seat, peering at the house. "How much trouble are we in?"

Leo grimaced. "A lot."

"They know we left."

"Well, they'd have found out anyway, since Valerian is here. It's not like we could just take him out of our closet and yell *surprise*."

Valerian snorted from the backseat. "Should Cooper and I leave?" he asked.

Leo shook his head and opened his door. "You're not going anywhere. Elijah won't be happy, but he'll reserve his anger for York and me. We'll be fine. I'm sure Albert is waiting for you, so we should go."

Leo quickly walked around the car to get to Valerian. Now that Leo didn't have to focus on their surroundings, he could help the psychic more easily than York. He was taller and more muscled and hadn't been underfed like York.

The house door flew open as they left the car behind and headed toward it. Leo held his breath when people streamed out, hoping they wouldn't overwhelm Valerian. It was probably a lost cause, and he realized he was right as soon as

Marcel's mother pushed her way toward York. York stared at her with wide eyes that went even wider when she threw her arms around his neck.

"I was so worried," she said, squeezing him tight.

He looked at Leo, who shrugged. Leo saw him tighten his arms around Marcel's mother, but he couldn't focus on them because Elijah made his way through the crowd until he stopped in front of him.

"I thought we'd agreed we'd go tomorrow," he said, giving Valerian a pointed glance.

Leo didn't want to throw York to the wolves or, as it was, to the dragons. "York was right. It would have been too dangerous for Valerian to be left behind longer than necessary."

"And you thought it was a good idea to sneak out of the house in the middle of the night and vanish? Corinne saw you leave, and she was frantic. We had to convince her that going after you was a bad idea."

"It was my fault," York said as he stepped closer. "I snuck out. I understand why you wanted to wait, but I didn't think we should, and I was right. Curt was coming to see Valerian again tonight. Taking him away means Curt won't be able to hurt him, and he's already been through enough."

Elijah turned his attention to Valerian, then gestured, and Albert appeared at his side. They looked worried, which Leo understood now that he could see Valerian better. He'd turned paler during his time in the car and looked like he might be about to faint.

"Welcome to our clan," Elijah told Valerian. "Albert is a doctor, and he'll take good care of you. You won't have to worry about a thing except getting better."

Valerian nodded. "Thank you. And please, don't punish Leo and York. I'm pretty sure I would have died if they hadn't come for me."

Elijah sighed, something he seemed to do a lot when York

was involved. "I won't punish them. Yell at them for a bit, yes, but no punishment. They did the right thing, and they're not bound by being a clan leader. I would have come for you sooner if I hadn't had to think of my clan first."

"I never expected anyone to put me first."

"Well, you do come first now, since as long as you agree, you're a clan member."

Cooper had let go of Valerian's hand, and Leo couldn't see him anywhere. He was sure Cooper was there, too, and he was glad York had his brother back. He was looking forward to getting to know both Cooper and Valerian, but right now, the thing he was looking the most forward to was dragging York to bed and sleeping for the next week.

Albert moved closer to Valerian, as did York. Leo could see it would take some time before he and York could go to bed. York would want to make sure Valerian was okay, and that was fine with Leo.

"Come," Albert said. "I don't think you need to go to the infirmary, but I can take you there if you'd feel more comfortable in a medical setting. If you're fine with a guest bedroom, though, I'm sure you'll be more comfortable there."

Valerian smiled. "A guest room would be perfect."

York took over from Leo, helping Valerian to the front door. Leo watched them go, but he knew Elijah would want to talk to him before he could follow, so he stayed where he was. The crowd started to disperse, and Leo waited.

"You scared us," Elijah said.

"I know, and I'm sorry."

Elijah snorted. "You're not."

"Well, not really. I think that York and I did the right thing, and I'd do it again if it meant saving Valerian."

"That's the only reason I'm not yelling at you. You might have done this the wrong way, but it was still the right thing. You couldn't let York do it on his own, and he was bent on going. Still, I wish you'd let me know."

"What would you have done? You'd have tried stopping us, and there was no stopping York. After seeing what I saw, I'm glad he pushed so hard."

Elijah looked at the house. "Valerian is in a rough state."

"That's an understatement. Curt's an asshole. He was beating him, and not just him." Leo thought back to Terrence. "There was a cockatrice shifter there. He was supposed to be a guard, but I'm pretty sure he and Valerian fell in love. He was beaten up pretty badly, probably because of York's disappearance, and I wouldn't be surprised if Curt beat him again now that Valerian is gone. He couldn't come with us because of his family, but I told him he'd be welcome if he found us."

Elijah stared at Leo. "You're offering our clan to every stray you find."

Leo grinned. "I don't see how that's a bad thing. They deserve a home, all of them. They deserve a family, to be happy, and to do what they want with their life. You and I were lucky enough to be born in the clan and have all the opportunities in the world. Is it so bad that I want to give York, Valerian, and others the same?"

Elijah shook his head. "Of course not. A cockatrice shifter, though?"

"Not every cockatrice shifter is an asshole like Curt or their alpha. I don't know Terrence, but Valerian does, enough that he fell in love with him. Surely, that means something."

"How about I agree to give this cockatrice shifter a chance if he comes? I'm not making promises, considering he's a cockatrice, but I'll talk to him at the very least."

"That's fine." It would have to be. Leo couldn't even be sure Terrence would manage to leave the cockatrices. He cared for his family, and they'd be welcome here, too, but Leo knew nothing about them. He didn't know why it seemed so impossible for Terrence to leave.

He hoped he'd find out eventually. He'd been angry at Terrence, but now that every person he cared about was safe, he couldn't find it in himself to hold on to that anger. If anything, he felt pity for Terrence. Leo had everything he'd ever wanted in life, while Terrence had none of it. It wasn't fair.

"Can we go back to bed?" Gunter grumbled.

He was wearing the tiniest pair of shorts Leo had ever seen and a tank top that was cut wide under his armpits. He'd wrapped his arms around himself, but he was still shivering, which made sense considering how cold it was.

Leo's eyes widened when Elijah stepped closer to Gunter and wrapped an arm around his shoulders. "I'll walk you back to your bedroom," he murmured.

Leo watched them go. He didn't know what the future would hold for him, York, Valerian, or Cooper, but they were a family, which meant they'd support each other. Elijah was probably right when he said that the war with the cockatrices was inevitable, but the longer they managed to hold it off, the better it would be. Valerian and York needed to recuperate after what Curt had done to them, and if at all possible, they needed to find out what Curt was planning.

Before he put it into motion.

York wasn't surprised when Albert led them to the guest wing where he had his own bedroom. He hadn't slept there the past few nights, but it would be good to be close to Valerian in case Valerian needed anything. York couldn't help Albert, but he could fetch the things Valerian would need for the night.

First, he helped Valerian sit on the bed. Valerian looked around, almost as if he was afraid he'd be locked up in this bedroom, too. York patted his hand, trying to reassure him.

"The door won't be locked, at least not from outside. You can lock it from the inside if you want. There are clothes in the drawers in various sizes, so you should be able to find something that fits you. That door there is the bathroom." This bedroom was almost identical to the one York had been set up in. "As soon as Albert confirms he doesn't need me, I'll go downstairs to grab you some food."

"Nothing heavy," Albert said. He was already focused on Valerian. "You haven't been eating much."

Valerian shook his head. "More toward the end, when I started trusting the man cooking my meals, but he didn't have much to work with. I suspect he was the one buying the food for me, and he did what he could with the little he had."

York hadn't realized that Terrence had been the one buying and cooking the food. It wasn't a surprise, though. Curt didn't take care of people, not even when they could be useful to him.

Albert nodded. "I see. York, if you can find some soup, that would be great. Water, too. If Valerian can keep all of that down during the night, he can have something more substantial tomorrow morning for breakfast."

"Anything else?" York asked, looking from Albert to Valerian.

"It'll take me a little while to examine Valerian. I'll help him in the shower once I'm done, so take your time," Albert said, not even looking at York.

York wasn't offended. Besides, he wanted to give Valerian space and privacy, so it would be best if he left the room. Cooper was hovering in the corner, and York was dying to talk to him, but Valerian's health came first.

"I'll be back soon," he promised as he slipped out of the room and closed the door behind himself.

Cooper appeared next to him, startling him. They stared at each other, and even though they couldn't touch now that

183

Valerian wasn't with them, it was tempting to reach for him.

"I don't know how to thank you," Cooper said.

"You don't have to."

"You saved his life. He's—he's everything to me. When I died, I had no idea what had happened to me. He didn't know, either, but he was there for me when I was lost. I don't know what would have happened if it weren't for him, and I don't ever want to find out."

"You won't have to. He's safe now, and the clan will take care of him. Of you, too, if you need anything."

"I just need for him to be safe."

"He is," York promised. "The clan kept me safe, even after what I did. You don't have to worry about Valerian."

Cooper finally relaxed. "Touching you was incredible."

"It was, and I can't wait to be able to hug you."

"Same."

"Do you think Valerian will want to stick around, then?" Because if Valerian left, so would Cooper, and York didn't want that to happen. There was also the Terrence thing, but York didn't think this was the right moment to ask his brother about the cockatrice.

"We're not going anywhere," Cooper said with a smile. "And not just because I never want to lose you again."

"Terrence?"

Cooper nodded. "It's complicated, but he's important to both of us."

"That's enough for him to be important to me. I don't know if Elijah will agree to send someone to get him, but we can ask."

Cooper shook his head. "It's no use. Even if Elijah does send someone, Terrence won't come. He has his family to think about."

"But he also has you."

"He'll follow us as soon as he can."

Cooper sounded like he was trying to convince himself, and York hoped he was right. It didn't matter to him that his brother had seemingly fallen in love with two different men. He just wanted Cooper to be happy. He could date a dozen men, and York wouldn't care.

"I'm going downstairs to grab some food for Valerian. Why don't you come with me? You can explore the house a bit."

"Thank you for taking care of him."

"He's yours, which means he's mine, too."

"The same goes for Leo, then."

York smiled. "I suppose it does. I'm glad that he can see you, even if it's only when Valerian is around."

"I was happy to meet him. I'm glad you found your way in life, even though you didn't do it like I expected. I'm sorry you had to go through all of that on your own. I should have been with you."

"You died, so I don't blame you for not being by my side. We don't have to worry about any of this anymore, though. You and Valerian are safe, and you're here. I'm sure Terrence will follow soon. Then, we'll take care of Curt together, and we'll finally be able to live our lives." It sounded too good to be true, and York was making it much simpler than it actually was, but he believed everything he'd said.

Before, he'd thought he'd lost every reason to live. His brother had been dead, and he'd been alone, homeless, with no opportunities to change his life. Meeting Curt had been the worst thing that could have happened to him, yet at the same time, it had also been the best. Through Curt, he'd met Marcel, then the clan and Leo. Through them, he'd gotten Cooper back.

They had all their lives in front of them to be happy, and even longer when it came to Cooper since he was dead. York wouldn't be comfortable until he was sure Curt was out of the picture, but getting Valerian and Cooper back was a good beginning.

And for the first time, he was eager to find out what happened next. He was eager to help, change the world, and make sure Curt couldn't hurt anyone else.

EPILOGUE

The coolness and hardness of the stone bench under York's ass were familiar, as was the ghost sitting next to him. Cooper hadn't been a ghost the last time they'd sat together like this, but what he was or wasn't didn't matter. As long as they could be together, talk and be a family like before, York was happy.

He thought Cooper was, too.

Things were settling down. It had been a few days since Cooper and Valerian had moved in with the clan, and while Valerian was still in bed, resting and healing, Cooper had started exploring the house. He'd spent almost as much time with York as he had with Valerian, and it warmed York's heart to know how much his brother cared about him. He wanted to give Cooper the world, especially after he'd lost so much, but unfortunately, he had no way to make that happen. He couldn't even give Valerian and Cooper Terrence, although he'd been thinking about how to help the three of them.

"I can't believe everything that happened," Cooper said, looking around.

"It'll probably take you a while. When I first arrived here, I expected the dragons to kill me. I wouldn't have blamed them, either. What I did to Marcel was unforgivable."

"Yet they welcomed you," Cooper pointed out.

"I was lucky they did. I'm still not sure I deserve their forgiveness, but I'm glad I have it. Without them, I wouldn't have you back." York's eyes prickle with tears, but they were happy ones this time.

Cooper reached for York, but he couldn't touch him. His hand went through York's arm, making him shiver at the sudden cold. They both laughed, and even though something in York's chest squeezed at the thought that his brother couldn't touch him, it wasn't a disaster.

They'd talk in Valerian's room, and they'd be able to hug again.

Hugging Cooper was everything York had thought he'd never have again. He'd never take it for granted, just like he wouldn't take the clan and everything they'd done for granted. Most days, it was hard to believe this was his life now, but he wouldn't change it for anything in the world.

Cooper got to his feet. "I should probably go check on Valerian."

"Wasn't he sleeping when you left the bedroom?"

"He was, but he has nightmares."

York grimaced. "I can understand that."

"Unfortunately, so can I. That's why I'm glad I don't have to sleep." Cooper hesitated. "You'll be all right?"

"I'll be fine. Leo is around here, so if I need anything, I'll call him."

Cooper nodded. "All right. I'll see you soon."

Those were the last words Cooper had told York the day he died. He'd died soon after, and York had lost him for too long. They'd see each other soon this time, and that certainty made York want to cry. Gosh, he was so emotional lately. No one blamed him, considering everything that happened, but sometimes, he felt like he spent more time crying than doing anything else.

He sat on his bench for a while longer, knowing Leo was probably hovering around, giving him time. He smiled when he heard the leaves on the ground crackle as Leo walked toward him. He looked up, and Leo had never been so beautiful, even though he was wearing a pair of jeans with holes and a dirty sweater.

"Everything okay?" Leo asked as he stopped next to the bench. "Is Cooper here?"

"He went back to Valerian. You can sit with me."

Leo had taken to always asking if Cooper was around and was sitting down. Now that he'd seen him, he'd explained it was weird for him to think he might be sitting in Cooper's lap. It had made everyone laugh, including Cooper, who kept trying to sneak in seats ahead of Leo now. The problem was that unless Cooper was touching Valerian, Leo couldn't see him, and Cooper wasn't solid, so Leo never knew he was there.

Leo sat and held out his hand. There was dirt under his nails, but York didn't care. He linked their fingers together, squeezing hard. "I'm all right," he promised.

"I know. It's just a lot to get used to."

"It is." And that was without even considering Curt.

The clan had no way of knowing how he'd reacted to both York and Valerian vanishing until they sent Kenneth in, but it couldn't be good, and they didn't know if the cockatrices had another psychic somewhere, so they weren't willing to risk it for now. York could see the worry in Valerian and Cooper's expressions, and he wished he could do something for Terrence. Unfortunately, Valerian and Cooper agreed that Terrence wouldn't come unless he could get his family to come with him, which wouldn't be easy. York hadn't asked why, but he wondered if maybe he should.

"We'll face everything together," Leo promised.

York leaned against his side, and Leo unlinked their fingers so he could wrap an arm around York's shoulders. He held him close, and York breathed in and out a few times. "I'm worried about Terrence."

"So am I, but I don't think there's anything we can do. We'll be ready when he comes, though."

"What about Curt?"

"Whatever he was planning, I'm pretty sure that losing you and Valerian will slow him down. Hopefully, he'll have a hard time finding another mage psychic. Or is that psychic mage?"

York laughed. "You'd have to ask Valerian. You really think Curt got set back?"

"He's still hiding with the cockatrices. He was there before, too, when he was trying to convince Valerian to work for him. That means that whatever he's planning, he needs a mage psychic. I don't think they grow on trees, so it'll probably take him a while to find another one, especially one as powerful as Valerian. Hopefully, it will be months, if not longer."

"But eventually, he'll strike," York whispered.

Leo's arm tightened around York, and he kissed the top of his head. "He will, but when he does, we'll face him together. We'll face him as a family and a clan, and we'll win."

York had to believe they would.

He wouldn't have it any other way.

ABOUT THE AUTHOR

Catherine is the creator of several series, most of them paranormal, including the Whitedell Pride Series and the Gillham Pack Series. While she graduated in translation, she decided to go the writer's way because it was more fun to create her own stories and characters.

She's been living in Italy for more than twenty years, but she's a daughter of the North—Belgium to be precise—and she misses it so much that she's already planning to move back.

She loves pizza—probably too much—her son, her pets, and of course, books. She sneaks some reading time into her schedule every time she has five minutes free from writing, demands from her various pets and son, and lastly, housework.

Connect with her:

lievens.catherine@gmail.com
BookBub: https://www.bookbub.com/authors/catherine-lievens
Website: https://authorcatherinelievens.com/
Facebook: https://www.facebook.com/catherine.lievens.9
Facebook Group: https://www.facebook.com/groups/411778002341528/
Twitter: https://twitter.com/authorCLievens
Newsletter: http://eepurl.com/c-uvKn

www.ingramcontent.com/pod-product-compliance
Lightning Source LLC
Chambersburg PA
CBHW060813120626
46557CB00001B/195